After making a diplomatic pac
other leaders of the Elder Ra
Dragos Cuelebre, Lord of the
Hollywood to spend a week with the Light Fae Queen,
Tatiana, before the busy Masque season hits New York
in December.

Dragos has never let the lack of an invitation stop him
from doing anything he wanted. Unwilling to let his mate
make the trip without him, he travels to southern
California in secret to be with her.

But when an ancient enemy launches a shattering assault
against the Light Fae, Dragos and Pia must intercede.
The destruction threatens to spread and strike a mortal
blow against all of the magically gifted, both human and
Elder Race alike.

Working with the Light Fae to neutralize the danger,
Dragos and Pia find their deepest vulnerabilities chal-
lenged and their most closely held secrets threatened
with exposure.

PIA DOES HOLLYWOOD is the second part of a
three-story series about Pia, Dragos, and their son, Liam.
Each story stands alone, but fans might want to read all
three: DRAGOS GOES TO WASHINGTON, PIA
DOES HOLLYWOOD, and LIAM TAKES MAN-
HATTAN.

Pia Does Hollywood

(A Story of the Elder Races)

Thea Harrison

Pia Does Hollywood
Copyright © 2015 by Teddy Harrison LLC
ISBN 10: 0990666174
ISBN 13: 978-0-9906661-7-2
Print Edition

Cover Art © Frauke Spanuth

Chapter One

DRAMATIC MUSIC EBBED and swelled on the widescreen TV.

"Here it comes," said Liam, poking Pia in the ribs with an insistent finger. "One of my favorite zombie movie quotes ever. Wait for it...."

For Halloween that year, Liam had set a goal to watch (and in some cases rewatch) all the zombie movies available for rental or purchase. Halloween had since come and gone, and now, in early November, he had fallen behind, but he was still determined to persevere until he had finished all of them.

The young actor came on the screen. Pia couldn't remember the guy's name.

Then Liam said along with the actor, "In those moments where you're not quite sure if the undead are really dead, dead, don't get all stingy with your bullets."

When he finished, he cackled.

She ran her fingers through his honey blond hair, relishing his cheerful mood. "You have the whole movie memorized, don't you?"

His dancing violet-blue gaze slid to hers. "Of course."

"Why do you like that line more than any of the others?" she asked curiously. "It's a pretty funny movie."

Actually, in truth, she wasn't a big fan of zombie movies, but she also wasn't about to tell Liam that. If this was what he wanted to do, why then, she wanted to do it with him.

Their lives were busy and demanding, and took them away from Liam too much as it was. And childhood was so brief and fleeting at the best of times, but even more so for Liam, as he grew at such a fast rate. As a result, she threw herself into everything he wanted to do with complete enthusiasm. No reservations—she was all in, every time.

"I *do* like all the rest of it," Liam said, his gaze cutting back to the television screen. "I just don't want to quote too much while it's playing, so you can enjoy the movie too."

My good, sweet boy, she thought. Even when he's acting like an adorably normal, obnoxious kid, he tries to be considerate.

They lay on the carpeted floor together, their bodies making a *T*. Pia stretched out parallel to the couch where Dragos lounged, one leg draped off the couch, his foot planted on the floor.

Dragos was working on his laptop and half watching the movie along with them. Pia rested one hand around his ankle, enjoying the simple, tactile contact. Liam lay facing the TV with his head propped on her abdomen as a pillow.

Outside the family room windows, the November

weather had turned sharp and cold as a wet, slushy mixture of rain and snow fell, but inside, they were warm and cozy. A fire crackled in the fireplace, filling the place with soft golden light. Pia had a cup of hot cocoa, made with coconut milk, that sat cooling on a coaster on one of the end tables, but she was too comfortable and happy to move.

At least not yet. She would have to move soon enough.

As the Cuelebres' part of the diplomatic deal they had made last month with the other Elder Races demesnes and the human government, later that evening she would be taking the company jet to fly to Los Angeles to visit with the Light Fae Queen, Tatiana, for a week.

The diplomatic deal stated that each of the seven U.S. demesne leaders was supposed to send a family member to another demesne to visit for a week to *foster good will and peace among the demesnes'*. The whole concept came from a Medieval practice of nobles sending their children to live in other nobles' households as hostages.

Supposedly, the diplomatic pact would lessen the likelihood of inter-demesne violence in the modern day United States, but whatever human idiot in the president's administration had thought up the scheme didn't really know jack shit about the Elder Races, their long memories, and their proclivity for holding grudges over centuries.

A week's visit wasn't going to fix anything. In fact, depending on how well or badly that family representative acted, it could very well cause more resentments and bad feelings between the demesnes. Or even outright war.

Also, it couldn't have come at a worse time. They had so much to do to get ready for the massive Masque that Dragos hosted in New York on the winter solstice that preparations always began a few months early, so Pia wasn't going to be forgiving that anonymous fool in a hurry for proposing the idea.

Dragos, in fact, wanted to reject the pact outright. He wasn't a fan of decisions made by consensus. At the best of times, he fought to rein in his autocratic instincts whenever the seven demesne leaders needed to convene over anything, and he had especially opposed this particular arrangement. But in the end, Pia told him, it would be easier to acquiesce on this one issue than to dig in their heels.

She could have waited to go later, after the Masque and sometime early next year. In fact, Tatiana had even emailed her the previous day, suggesting that she come at a later date.

But when Pia thought of the reason why that option wasn't attractive, she lost her crankiness and began to smile.

All things considered, it was better for her to suck it up, get on the plane that night and get the damn visit over with, despite how much she dreaded spending the week with the Light Fae Queen and her nosy questions. So she emailed Tatiana back, thanked her for the suggestion, and said she would be touching down in L.A. the next morning as originally planned.

Dragos would be traveling to Los Angeles too, under separate cover. He didn't volunteer how he was going to make the trip, and she didn't ask. Probably he would relish the chance to stretch out his massive wings and fly cross-country in the darkness and solitude, but they had agreed—if she didn't know what he was doing, she could say with perfect sincerity that she had traveled alone to the Light Fae demesne.

After all, the best way to lie to someone with a highly developed truthsense was to, well, tell the truth. Pia believed wholeheartedly in plausible deniability, at least as much as possible.

After her exchange with Liam, she met Dragos's amused gaze, gave him a small nod, and squeezed his ankle. In answer, he closed his laptop as she said to Liam, "Hey sport, could you put the movie on pause for a few minutes?"

Instantly, Liam's sparkling smile vanished, and he scowled. "You said you could watch the whole movie with me before you left."

"I know I did, and I will watch the whole movie with you," she told him. "But first, your dad and I have something important we want to tell you."

Heaving a sigh, he held up the remote and hit pause. "What is it now?"

"Don't be pissy," Dragos told him. "And while you're readjusting your attitude, sit up and turn around."

Pia could feel Liam sigh again, but so far, he had been unwilling to challenge Dragos's authority when

Dragos used that particular tone with him. (And lordy, wouldn't life get interesting whenever Liam did decide to challenge Dragos and rebel.)

As the boy pushed to a sitting position and swiveled to face the couch, Pia sat too and leaned back against Dragos's legs.

As Dragos dropped a large, warm hand onto her shoulder, he asked her telepathically, *Do you want to be the one to tell him?*

She drew up her knees and wrapped her arms around them, hugging herself with glee. *It's okay with me either way. You can tell him if you want.*

Okay. Dragos switched to verbal speech. "Liam, we're pregnant. You're going to have a new sibling."

For the space of a moment, Liam's expression went blank with surprise.

He held still just long enough that Pia had time to rethink their decision. She and Dragos had kept the news to themselves for a few weeks, which was easy to do since the new little peanut appeared to be determined to keep his—or her—presence a secret. Only Pia's doctor and Eva knew the truth, and only because Pia had collapsed last month during their trip to Washington for the Elder Races/human summit meetings.

But what if Liam reacted poorly, for some reason? What if he wasn't happy with the news? They were dropping a big bombshell on him then leaving for a week, so they wouldn't be around to help him work through any of his emotions.

Anxiously, she twisted her hands together and came

to a fast decision. If he reacted poorly, she was going to override his decision to stay home and in school. She would make him come to L.A. with her. Somehow, she would juggle things so that she would get some time alone with him.

Then Liam's expression changed into one of pure joy. "Oh wow, really? Are you kidding me?" he exclaimed. "You mean I'm not going to be the only one anymore? That's fantastic!"

Thank the gods. Her face broke into a beam as she nodded. "Yes, we're pregnant. Really, truly!"

He dove forward to sprawl on his stomach and put his hand on her abdomen. "When did it happen? Is it going to be a brother or a sister? Can I feel it?"

"Be careful," she said quickly. When he tilted his head to look up at her, she told him, "Yes, you can try to sense it, but you have to be super gentle so you don't scare it. He—or she—is cloaking pretty hard. That could just be part of its nature, or maybe I frightened it. We got pregnant when we went to D.C., and I was pretty stressed that week."

She tried not to obsess over what had happened last month when they had traveled to Washington to participate in a summit between the leaders of the Elder Races and the human government, but the thought that she might have frightened that new, tiny spark bothered her quite a bit. Between the anti-Elder Races sentiment, the occasional outright hostility, the vice president's husband being murdered at their house during a very important dinner party and Pia's subsequent collapse, it had been one of the roughest weeks she had ever lived through.

Liam frowned. "I don't remember being frightened, and from all the stories you've told me, you were pretty stressed when you got pregnant with me too."

"You have a point." She wanted to believe him badly and bit her lip. "I know you've said before that you didn't pay attention to much of what happened outside your own experience, except the time that Urien shot me."

The time she—they—had almost died. Then, Liam, who had been nothing more than a peanut himself, had flared up to try to heal her, until Dragos laid his Power over the bright, new little spark and gentled him down.

A good thing, too, Dragos murmured in her head. *Considering all the rampant sex we had.*

Laughter flared, and she looked over her shoulder at him with dancing eyes. *And continue to have.*

"Yeah, that's right," Liam said, resting his cheek on her leg. "I remember sleeping a lot. Man, those were the best naps. I just sorted of drifted, weightless. And I remember feeling like you were so big, you were my entire universe. Which I guess you were."

She ran her fingers through his hair again. "And you felt safe?"

"Totally safe, except that once." His smile faded only briefly then returned. "Then I remember Dad being there, and I was safe again."

Relief coursed through her. Dragos's fingers tightened gently on her shoulder. She reached up to stroke his long, warm fingers as she said, "Okay, if this peanut is anything like you were, then what was happening in my reality won't really impinge on his—or her—awareness. Agh, these pronouns are going to be hard to juggle until we know the sex of the baby. Anyway, it must be cloaking itself out of instinct, so that's part of its nature."

"Can you sense it now?" Liam asked.

"I can, but your dad had to show me how at first. And he only knew because Dr. Medina told us I was pregnant," she replied. "Want me to show you?"

He nodded, and when he sank his bright, familiar Power into her body—gods, Liam was every bit as strong as Dragos—she brushed her awareness against his and told him telepathically, *Ease up a little there. You're feeling pretty intense.*

Sorry! he said. *I'm just excited.*

I know. I am too. When his presence lightened, she guided him to the subtle, tiny shadow, and together they hovered to observe it.

After a few moments, it occurred to her that Liam had unique capabilities that were quite different from anything she, Dragos or Dr. Medina had.

She asked him curiously, *This little shadow is all any of us can pick up. Can you sense anything?*

Once again, he took his time in responding, and she held her breath as she waited for his reply.

Finally, he said, *I'm not sure. As I watch it, I keep getting impressions of fire.*

Fire? she repeated. *I guess that would make sense. Both you and your dad are pretty fiery.*

She felt rather than saw, Liam shake his head. *No, I'm not quite the same as Dad. I don't think I'm as hot as this one is. This one feels as hot as Dad does, to me.*

Oh wow, was she going to have another dragon baby? The suspense was going to kill her!

Hugging herself tighter, she told herself she wasn't going to ask it, but then immediately she caved and asked it anyway. *Can you sense if it's a boy or a girl?*

This time, he answered her quickly. *No, I'm not picking anything else up. Just heat and fire.*

Well, that's more than your dad and I have been able to sense so far. How exciting! As Liam's presence pulled away, she surfaced with him. They grinned at each other.

"You both look like a pair of Cheshire cats," Dragos told them. He was smiling as well.

"Tell him what you saw." She poked Liam in the stomach. "Tell him!"

He was very ticklish, and his lanky body folded around her prodding finger as he laughed. "I'm not sure I saw anything!"

"You did too," she insisted. Twisting to look at Dragos, she told him, "He did too."

"You've got good instincts," Dragos told Liam. "Trust them. What was it?"

"I just kept getting impressions of fire," Liam said to his father. "That's all. It felt hotter than I do, more like you."

"Ah," said Dragos, with intense male satisfaction. "That sounds like it could be another dragon."

"You don't know that." Pia waved a cautioning finger in the air. "It could mean a fiery nature."

"True." He captured her finger, pulled her hand to him and kissed the finger. "But I doubt Liam would just sense a hothead. My guess is, whether the baby is a dragon or not, Liam is somehow reading the new one's Power."

Laughing, Liam held up both hands. "I don't know anything for sure! Maybe I imagined it. I just think it's so cool I'm going to have a baby brother or sister. Maybe it'll be like me in some ways!"

Did that statement carry a hint of loneliness in it? Always hypersensitive to the possibility, Pia's heart clutched at the thought.

So many things served to isolate him. He had so little in common with other children. He was growing up so fast, he couldn't make lasting friends, and he was the prince of his people, with both unusual dangers and unusual privilege. And as he said, his nature was not like his father's; Dragos was, at heart, a solitary creature. Liam loved people.

In the next instant, the feeling melted into another warm glow of happiness. If Liam had felt any kind of loneliness at being an only child with such a unique nature, this new little one had already eased it.

Dragos said quietly, "I think you need to leave. Right now, the temps haven't dropped below freezing, but I want you safely in the air and well away from here before ice develops on the runway. There's more than an hour left to the movie—you'll have to watch the rest of it after the trip after all."

Even though Liam had responded to the news so much better than she had feared that he might, she still felt reluctant to let go of the moment.

Turning back to Liam to search his dark blue gaze, she said, "You can always change your mind and come too, you know. You sure you want to stay here? It'll be sunny and warm in L.A. And while I can't promise, we might be able to sneak away for an afternoon at Disneyland, if you want."

"No," he said. "I'd like to go to Disneyland someday, but I'd like to go some time when you know you can make the trip. This week, I really want to stay in school. We have a football game on Friday night. I want to play in it, and besides, you said this is the last trip you're gonna be making for a while. And you'll be back by next Monday, right?"

"That's right," she replied. "I'll be home on Monday by the time school lets out."

He shrugged. "Okay. Do you want to watch the rest of the movie with me when you get back?"

"Of course I do." She leaned over to poke him in the ribs again. "Unless you want to go ahead and finish it tonight, which is okay too. If you watch the rest of it, we can start a new movie when I get back."

"Okay." He laughed and squirmed away from her finger. "And hey, maybe by the time you get back, this peanut won't be hiding anymore."

"You never know." She grinned. "Peanuts do tend to have a mind of their own. But you were 'Peanut' when you were little. Do you think we need to come up with another nickname to call this one?"

"Nah," Liam said. "I outgrew that a long time ago, so we can call this one Peanut too."

She looked sideways away from him, adopting a shifty expression. "Does that mean I get to have your bunny now?"

"No way!" he exclaimed. "Keep your paws off my stuffed animal!"

Laughing, she told him, "I'll keep my hands off him for now. That's all I'm going to promise. If you ever feel the need to get rid of him, you know he's got a home with me."

"Yeah, I know." He grinned.

Behind her, Dragos shifted. "Time to get this trip started. The sooner you leave, the sooner we can put this week behind us and move on with our lives."

Taking his cue, she rolled onto her knees and stood. Liam stood as well.

Pia called out, "Eva!"

After a few moments, Eva appeared in the doorway. "You bellowed?"

"Pia's ready to leave for the airstrip," Dragos told her. "Is the Escalade loaded up?"

"It sure is." Eva bounced on the balls of her feet. "We're ready to roll as soon as you are."

He nodded. "Get the car warmed up and wait for us outside, will you? We'll be out soon."

"Sure thing." Eva disappeared down the hall.

Pia turned to Liam. Good gods, he was almost as tall as she was. She said, "Remember …"

He ducked his head with a self-conscious grin. "I know, I know. No unexpected growth spurts while you're gone."

She waited a moment when he stopped speaking, then prompted, "And?"

"We'll Skype every day after school." He added quickly, "Except for Friday, because there's the game. And Hugh's going to tape it, so you can watch it when you get back."

"That's what we're going to do, first thing after school on Monday," Dragos told him. "We'll watch it together."

"Okay!"

Pia watched as Liam hugged Dragos. When he turned to her, she was ready. She threw her arms around him and kissed his cheek. He whispered to her, "I'm so glad I get to have a Peanut too."

"Me too, darling." She kissed him again. "I just know he—or she—is going to look up to you and adore you, and want to play with you all the time."

"I can't wait. I'll even learn how to change diapers!" His brows twitched together, and he added, "As long as they're not poopy."

She burst out laughing. "Wow, that is excessively good of you."

He kissed her cheek quickly and stood back. "Have a good trip!"

"We will," she told him. Liam threw his thin, lanky body onto the empty couch and turned the movie back on as they walked out of the room.

Then, as Pia followed Dragos to the front of the shadowed house, she said to him, "Unless, of course, we don't. Because I swear to you, Dragos, I'm beginning to feel like we're travel cursed. Something always happens when we go away."

"Like I told you once, we're lightning rods. We don't have to go away for things to happen," he said sardonically. At the front hall closet, he pulled out Pia's coat. "Things happen when we stay right here at home too."

She would not look at the thin white scar on his forehead. She had obsessed over that wound more than enough already. A few months ago, when Dragos had been seriously injured, that wound had ruled her life and haunted her nights.

Now, he still suffered partial memory loss, but he had remembered everything that mattered to her, everything that was vital to their lives and happiness. More importantly, he had healed until he was as strong and healthy as he had ever been.

And they were going to have a new, mysterious, fiery little peanut.

So she patted him on the cheek as she told him, "I'm too stinking happy to care. The universe can bring it. We'll deal with whatever may happen next. We always do."

He bent his head to kiss her. "Damn straight, and we always will."

The kiss quickly turned scorching as he slanted his mouth over hers and deepened it, cupping the back of her head and plunging between her lips with his tongue.

She stroked his hair, savoring the feeling of the silken strands flowing through her fingers and the sensation of his warm, firm lips caressing hers.

He had been drinking coffee while watching the movie, and the dark, smoky flavor lingered pleasantly on his tongue. Murmuring in pleasure, she kissed him back hungrily.

The mating frenzy between them had flared when they began to try to get pregnant. Now, only a few short weeks later, it had eased back somewhat but it hadn't gone to sleep entirely.

Pia was beginning to think it never would. She could never get enough of him, never, and now, if they weren't able to steal away for a few private hours, it was likely they wouldn't be able to be together for a whole damn week, which was another reason to hold a grudge against that unnamed idiot in Washington.

Dragos lifted his head, and in the shadows of the front hall, his gold eyes flared incandescent. He looked hungry, and angry. It was all the warning she got.

Grabbing her by the waist, he lifted her into his arms. Laughing and trying to muffle the sound, she managed to hook an arm around his neck as he strode the short distance to his office.

"What are you doing?!" she whispered, breathless from trying to hold back her giggles.

"I'm taking my wife." Slamming the door with one booted foot, he carried her to the massive desk and swept everything out of the way as he set her on the polished surface.

Her body knew what was coming next. Her pulse rate ratcheted up, until she felt she had a fever, and a hungry ache throbbed in the private place between her legs. "I thought we didn't have time for this."

"Screw it," he growled. "We'll make time."

Chapter Two

DRAGOS KNEW HE was throwing off heat as if he were on fire. He felt like he was burning up. He loved the fact that she never minded his heat. When they were in bed, she cuddled close, even in the warmest weather.

She spread slender hands across his chest. Her plump, inviting lips were unsteady as she whispered, "What about the roads?"

"They won't freeze in the next ten minutes." Undoing the fastening of her jeans, he hauled them and her panties off, taking her slip-on shoes with them. Then he yanked her legs apart.

She burst out laughing again. "Eva's outside in the car!"

"She knows her job," he muttered. "She'll wait."

Dragos knew when he got like this, there was no reasoning with him.

But fortunately, when he got like this, there was no reasoning with her either.

She didn't waste any more precious time arguing, not when he could tell she wanted this as much as he did. Arousal perfumed her scent. He took in deep breaths, gripping her shoulders as she worked to get his jeans open too.

When she did, and his stiff, aching erection spilled into her waiting hands, they both sucked in a breath.

It was a terrible thing to grow to need someone the way that he had grown to need her. For so many millennia, he had been content to be a solitary creature. The dragon in him was baffled by the unrelenting drive he felt to be with her, and stupefied at the experience of being in love.

Because he did, he loved her. He didn't love often, or very many people, and he was content to have it that way, but she consumed his life. She burned him up, until there was nothing left but his essence, taken out of his massive body and flying weightless again in the endless, unmeasured spill of profligate golden sunlight, just as he had once flown in the earliest days of his very long life.

Their lack of time lent urgency to their actions. She pumped his cock once, twice, three times, spiking sensation along his nerve endings until he could have spilled right then and there into her welcoming hands, but he didn't want to climax that way. He wanted to bury himself into her velvety soft, tight sheath.

As he yanked her soft sweater up, she obligingly raised her arms. Shimmering pale blonde hair tumbled over her laughing, sensual expression. He tossed the sweater to the floor and greedily filled his palms with her round, soft breasts, framed prettily by a cream lacy bra. Bending his head, he licked and bit lightly at the luscious swell of flesh. When he put his mouth over one nipple and sucked at her teasingly, through the material of the bra, she moaned and hooked her legs around his waist, trying to pull him close.

It was impossible—he couldn't suckle at her breasts and still come up to nestle against her pelvis. After a last hard pull and nip at her breast, he gave up, straightened and put an arm around her hips to pull her to the edge of the desk.

As she wriggled eagerly into position, he put a hand between her legs, fingering her soft, delicate folds. She was wet for him, but he already knew that from the arousal in her scent. Relishing the liquid glide of velvet flesh against his callused fingertips, he probed until he found the tight, stiff little pearl he was looking for.

She sucked in an unsteady breath as he caressed her, tightening her fists in the material of his shirt. He could feel the muscles in her inner thighs shaking against his hips. For a few moments, she thrust her pelvis against his hand, mimicking the rhythm they found when they were joined together, until his blood caught the rhythm, pulsing urgently through his veins.

Then she pushed his hand away, hissing, "Stop being so damn considerate and get inside me already, will you?"

Laughter welled up. Gods, he loved how frankly sensual she was with him, and her unabashed enthusiasm for sex.

She took hold of his cock again, rubbing her thumb along the broad sensitive head until moisture came out of the tip. Then she positioned him at her entrance, and gripping her hips, he pushed inside.

It never got old, never. Each time, he caught fire like it was the first time. When he planted himself deep inside her, she let her head fall back. Her gaze was unfocused, and her breathing came in short, quick pants.

Bending over her arched torso, one arm wrapped around her hips, he fucked her in short, hard jabs. The friction was excruciating, delicious. *She* was delicious. He bit at her neck, sucking at the delicate skin.

She raked her fingernails down his back, leaving trails of fire. Relishing the small pain, he growled and accelerated his pace. His erection felt huge, impossibly hard and thick. If he didn't spill soon, he was going to go crazy.

Slipping a hand between their torsos, he searched for her clitoris again—and as he connected with the tiny peak of flesh, she sucked in a breath, whined and climaxed. The ripples took her over. He could feel her pulsing around him, and that sent him over the edge.

Groaning, he pumped into her, jetting with each thrust. She bit and licked at him, until he lifted his head to take her mouth with his. They fused together, kissing wildly, muscles clenched as the last of the pleasure spiked and then eased on a slow ebb.

When it had passed, she wrapped her arms around his neck. He hugged her tightly, and they rested against each other for a moment until he felt her racing heart begin to slow.

"Okay," he said, as he rested his mouth in her tousled hair. "Now you can go."

Bursting out laughing, she smacked his arm. "After

you completely destroy me, mess up all my clothes and tangle my hair, you're going to boot me out?"

He grinned. "Well, I lost track, but I suspect our ten minutes might be up."

"Ugh, men!" Her hold on his neck loosened, and her thighs eased away from his hips.

Before he let her go, he had to take her chin and tilt her face up for one last hot kiss. Damn, he hated to let her go. "All right," he said reluctantly against her soft lips. "The half bath is right across the hall, and nobody's in the front of the house—you make a run for it while I straighten up your clothes. I'll bring them to you."

"Okay," she whispered. She stroked his face. In the shadowed room, her eyes looked dark as midnight and impossibly deep. She smiled at him. "I love you."

He kissed her again, hard. "Love you too. Get going, before I change my mind and keep you here."

She lingered to search his face. "You wouldn't."

"Damn straight, I would."

"But all the demesne leaders, and the human administration, agreed on this."

"Fuck them. Fuck the agreement." He angled out his jaw. "Nobody tells me what to do, or where to send my family."

OH LORD, HE was serious.

Only a few moments ago, while they were making love, he had looked so intense, he almost set the air around him on fire, his eyes glowing like gold coins in the darkened office.

Now he looked intense for an entirely different reason, and just as sexy. His dark brows had lowered, and his face had hardened into his most stubborn expression.

Shaking her head, she hopped off the desk. "I don't have time to argue with you about this," she told him. "We already decided—it's not worth antagonizing all the other people we have to live with on this continent over this one thing. You need to save all that obstinacy for times when you really do need to dig in your heels. If you're going to pick your battles, Dragos, this one isn't worth fighting."

He said between his teeth, "I *hate* decisions by consensus."

"I know," she crooned. "You handle it so much better when you can be an absolute dictator, don't you, honey? It's been very hard on you since the planet has become so populated, and we've all had to learn to get along together sometimes."

"Well," he said, his tone truculent. "It has."

Her shoulders shook. Gods, she adored every inch of his growly, autocratic self. "We've put it off long enough. Now I've really got to go."

Reluctance clear in every line of his body, he stepped aside, and she made that dash for the half bath across the hall.

Once inside, she cleaned up, washed her face and hands, and ran her fingers through her tousled hair. A quick rap sounded on the door, then Dragos opened it to slip her clothes inside, and she dressed quickly. She hopped out of the bathroom again in two minutes flat.

He was waiting for her, still glowering, holding her coat in one hand. As she shrugged into it, his arms closed around her tightly in one last hug. For that one moment, she felt entirely enfolded and utterly safe.

Then he let her go, and together they stepped outside.

The rainy snow splattered them as Dragos opened the front passenger door of the Escalade that waited idling at the curb. Inside, Eva lounged in the driver's seat, looking lazily amused and not at all surprised.

Pia turned to Dragos. Wet drops sprinkled his ink black hair.

"Do you have your next dose of medication?" he asked.

She nodded. "I've got it in my purse. I triple-checked."

"And I have the backup dose, just in case."

When she had collapsed in D.C., they had found out that she was pregnant. They had also discovered that this would be their last child.

It had to be, as Pia's body had developed lethal antibodies to fight off carrying Dragos's children. Sometimes it happened, when two very different kinds of Wyr mated.

Dr. Medina had likened it somewhat to the human Rhesus factor, only unlike humans, who could prevent dangerous sensitization with an injection of Rh immunoglobulin, there was no way to prevent what had happened to Pia.

Once her body had turned that corner, nothing in modern medicine could turn the clock back again. Not even her own magical nature could save her. While she had extraordinary healing Powers, her body had grown to recognize the fetus as an intruder and was fighting to protect itself. She would miscarry any future pregnancies.

She would be able to carry this new, precious peanut to term, but only with the help of the drug protocol that Dr. Medina had developed for her, in the form of a shot she had to take every two weeks.

Uneasy at being so vulnerable and dependent, after the first two doses, both Pia and Dragos had insisted they learn to give her the shot in case Dr. Medina wasn't available to administer it. Pia was due to have her next shot in two evenings.

Dragos touched her cheek gently with the callused tips of his fingers, lingering over the kiss. Then he pulled back and told her, "Have a good flight. I'll see you soon. I'll get in touch with you in the morning, after you've landed."

She nodded and gave him a smile. "Sounds good. Talk to you in the morning."

Eva put the car in gear while Dragos slammed the door.

As they drove away, Pia glanced back. Dragos never moved to go back inside. Instead, he stood watching her leave.

The next time they talked, it would be in secret in southern California. She watched him too, until his tall, dark figure and their glowing, inviting home faded into the darkness.

Only then did she turn to face the direction in which she was going. Belatedly, she realized she hadn't put on her seat belt, and with a muttered curse, she yanked the belt around her body and jammed it into the buckle.

"Good job being all reasonable with his lordship, dumbass," she muttered to herself. "If you'd only let him dig in his heels, you wouldn't be making this trip right now."

And to hell with the rest of the world.

"Anybody would think you really weren't going to see each other for a week," Eva said with a chuckle.

All her good mood from that evening vanished. Scowling, she crossed her arms and sank down in her seat. "You never know. The Light Fae demesne doesn't have an edict forbidding him to cross their borders like the Elven demesne did when we went to South Carolina, but he's still not supposed to be along for this trip. Even though he'll be in L.A. too and I'll be able to talk to him, I might not actually get a chance to see him for the whole week."

Eva shook her head. "I don't believe it. That man's too sneaky, and I mean that as a total compliment. If he wants to see you, he'll find a way to make it happen, whether he's supposed to or not. Only question is how he does it. I can't wait to see how he pulls it off."

Pia's scowl lifted and she began to smile. "You do have a point."

Chapter Three

P IA'S SECURITY TEAM had already boarded the plane. She heard the familiar arguing voices as she and Eva stepped into the cabin. Her astonished gaze took in Quentin and Aryal's presence as they sprawled on one of the couches.

The two sentinels looked lethal and relaxed, even as they sniped at each other. Quentin's sexy, scarred face wore a subtle amused expression, while Aryal scowled as she scratched a long-fingered hand through her tangled black hair.

Pia laughed out loud. "He never told me he was going to assign you two to the trip."

Quentin stood and stepped forward to press a kiss to her cheek. "He didn't want to say anything, in case you thought it might be a bad idea."

Aryal remained in her slouched position, one leg thrown over the arm of the couch, although she raised a few fingers in nonchalant greeting when Pia looked at her.

"No offense," Pia said, "but I do think it's a bad idea. While I love you two—yes, I've grown to love even you, Aryal—neither of you are known for your skills in diplomacy."

"That's not our job, cupcake," Aryal told her as she kicked one booted foot. "Diplomacy is your job. Our job is to make sure nobody kills you."

Within the space of five words, Aryal had already managed to get her irritated. No matter how many times Pia told her not to call her cupcake, the harpy persisted.

She threw up her hands. "Stop it. Nobody else but Graydon uses that nickname. Why do you keep calling me that?!"

Aryal's face went blank for a moment. Then, with a slightly baffled expression, she said, "It's—it's just so fitting. With your frothy blond hair, cute painted toenails and bright, pretty outfits, you *are* a cupcake."

Pia dropped her hands, lowered her chin and glowered at the harpy for a long moment. She said, "You're not even trying to be offensive right now, are you?"

Mutely, Aryal looked sidelong at Quentin as she shook her head. Eva had moved to the back of the cabin. As the other woman caught Pia's attention, Eva rolled her eyes.

Eva and Aryal couldn't stand each other. Pia had once said to Dragos that they were worse than oil and water. Eva was oil, and Aryal was a naked flame.

This wasn't just a bad idea. It was terrible.

Behind Pia, the door to the cockpit opened, and Alex, one of the two mated Wyr-ravens that worked as co-pilots, stepped into the cabin. "We're ready to take off when you are," he said, smiling at Pia. "The sooner the better, of course. The temperature outside is dropping fast."

Oh, for God's sake.

Pia turned her back to everyone else and looked at Alex. "You answer to me on this trip, correct?"

To his credit, Alex didn't look at the others either. "Yes, ma'am. You're the ranking Wyr official on board."

"Then we don't take off until I tell you to," Pia told him. She swiveled back to look at the other three. At the back of the cabin, Eva contemplated the ceiling with her generous lips pursed. Aryal had turned to inspecting her fingers, while Quentin's handsome expression grew more amused.

"My husband is an idiot," Pia declared.

Hey, Dragos said telepathically.

That meant he had followed the car to the airstrip. Dragos's hearing was very good, but even so, he had to be quite close to hear her through the plane's closed exterior. She imagined him in his dragon form, cloaking his presence as he paced impatiently around the jet, waiting for the engines to rev in preparation for taking off, and she had to suppress a smile.

If he was indeed in his dragon form and pacing around the plane, that meant he could look in through the windows and see her. She would not let him see that she was amused.

"Ma'am," said Alex. "We certainly won't take off until you say we can, but the weather has turned."

"Yes, I know it has," she said. She looked from Eva to Aryal and back again. "But I'm not going anywhere until I hear you all swear that you will get along on this trip and not cause me any headaches. Because guys, I don't need any of you with me in order to make the trip to L.A. I could kick you all off the plane and go to the Light Fae demesne by myself. In fact, that idea sounds pretty good to me. We're not at war with Tatiana. She'd look after me just fine."

In her head, the dragon gave a warning growl, while Quentin lost his smile. Aryal straightened and stood.

Quentin told her, "Pia, you can't go by yourself. That's ridiculous."

Crossing her arms, she retorted, "It's not as ridiculous as the alternative could be."

Because oil couldn't help but be oil. And a flame burned where it would. At some point, it was inevitable that the two would connect and explode. She gave both Eva and Aryal glances filled in equal parts with exasperation and affection.

"What's it going to be?" she asked. "Are you all going to get along on this trip and not give me any grief, or do I kick you all off the plane and go by myself.

You're not going by yourself, and that's final, Dragos growled.

Well, I know you're coming too, honey, she crooned.

That's not what I meant, Pia, he snapped. *I might be in L.A. too, but you need to have someone with you inside Tatiana's household as well.*

While Dragos thundered in her head, Quentin, Aryal and Eva all started to speak at once.

She clapped her hands over her ears and exclaimed, "Do you *see* what I'm talking about?! Arguing is exactly what I asked you not to do!"

"I'm only trying to point out that some of us might promise, but what if not everybody does?" Aryal snapped in reply. "Do you kick them off the plane, and keep the others? It's a legitimate question!"

As Eva glared at Aryal, Pia realized she was hearing more than Dragos growling in her head. Eva was growling too.

Because oil was oil. And flame couldn't help but be flame.

She would not laugh. She wouldn't. Instead, she rubbed the bridge of her nose and said pathetically to Dragos, *I'm supposed to avoid stress, you know.*

The dragon's growling stopped as abruptly as if she had turned it off like a faucet. When he next spoke, his voice was quiet and nonconfrontational. *I'm sorry, baby.*

That solved the issue of his growling. She turned her attention to Eva, and met the other woman's gaze silently. After a moment, Eva's low growl wavered and stopped. Eva said apologetically, *She makes me crazy.*

And I don't want to go visit the Light Fae demesne, Pia told her. *Deal with it like an adult or get off the plane. If you make this trip harder on me than it needs to be, I won't take you with me anywhere.*

Eva glared. *I wouldn't make it harder!*

Pia raised her eyebrows. *And so?*

Heaving an aggrieved sigh, Eva said out loud, "I promise to get along for the duration of this trip and not cause you any headaches."

"Thank you, Eva." She turned to Quentin and Aryal.

The amusement had crept back into Quentin's blue gaze. Pia could tell that he had figured out that while she was certainly serious, she wasn't really upset. He laid a hand over his heart and said, "Well, *I* promise, so that means I get to come too, right? I was looking forward to a sojourn in sunny SoCal, and Eva and I would be a fine pair of bodyguards for the week."

At that, everyone on the plane looked at Aryal, who had crossed her arms and wore a truculent expression. She angled her head to look at them all.

"So that's it," she said. "The whole trip is going to come down to this moment, isn't it? Agh, people make me crazy. If anything happens, everybody's going to say, 'oh, Aryal, you were the last one to promise. We all knew you were going to be a hassle. You always are.' Okay, okay! Of course I promise!"

Smiling, Quentin said to Pia, "She is the best, most perfect example of what a self-fulfilling prophecy is, isn't she? I just marvel at her every day."

Pia said to Dragos, *I am not going to forgive you for this in a hurry.*

It was a tactical decision, he told her. Did the dragon sound apologetic? Now, that was unusual. Pia was winning points all over the place. *I wanted you to have the strongest defense with the least number of bodies, and Quentin and Aryal work very well as a team.*

Uh huh. Pia walked over to Aryal and stuck a finger under her nose. Her finger was getting a lot of exercise that evening. She told the harpy aloud, "Do not make me regret taking you along. Because I can send you home from L.A. too, you know."

Aryal's mouth took on a sour tilt. With a quick side-long glance at her mate, she muttered, "Got it."

She nodded to herself and turned away, muttering to Dragos, *I still think this is a bad idea.* Aloud, she said, "Okay, Alex. Sorry for the holdup. Let's go."

"Yes, ma'am," Alex said cheerfully, and with evident relief.

THE NORMAL FLIGHT time from New York City to LAX was a smidgeon over six hours, but they were traveling from upstate New York to another private airstrip just outside of L.A., so their trip would be over seven hours.

Since she had the luxury of choosing, Pia had decided to deal with the long flight and subsequent jet lag by staying up a little later then traveling through the night, so that they would touch down at eight the next morning. With all the amenities that the jet provided, including good food, a comfortable place to nap, and the chance to shower, she expected to arrive alert and hopefully ready to face spending the week with the formidable Light Fae Queen.

After they had taken off, Alex's mate and co-pilot Daniel served them a late supper. Pia bolted her food down. So far this pregnancy was affecting her appetite as much as her last one had, and she was massively hungry all the time.

Thankfully, because the flight wasn't commercial and Cuelebre Enterprises owned the jet, the supper was outstanding and catered to her needs and personal tastes.

After an excellent meal of a savory sweet potato casserole, sautéed Brussel sprouts, a green salad, and lemon cake with raspberries for dessert, she stretched out on one of the couches with a blanket, slipped a black travel mask over her eyes and sank her awareness deep into her body where a small, subtle shadow rested.

I love you, she said to the shadow. *No matter who or what you are, I'll always love you. Precious little Peanut.*

Then, because probably the shadow didn't understand words, she tried to send all the love she had at it, as gently as she could. While she was doing that, she fell into a deep sleep.

The next thing she knew, she was climbing along her favorite trail in the Adirondacks, admiring the glorious fall colors as the trees turned brilliant red, orange and yellow.

She had been raised a city girl, because her mother believed that the best place for them to hide was in the middle of a dense, busy population. But part of Pia had always been wild, and one of the things she relished about moving to upstate New York was being able to sink into the outdoors without worrying about her safety. It soothed a part of her nature that had never before gotten the chance to stretch out her legs and roam.

Something rustled in the underbrush, and part of her attention turned to it, but she kept walking.

The slight rustle followed.

Pausing, she bent to pretend to tie her shoe. As she did so, she studied either side of the trail carefully.

Deep in the shadows of nearby brush, gold eyes

watched her.

Small gold eyes, close to the ground. She raised her eyebrows. There was no way that could be Dragos.

She started to smile. "It's okay if you want to come out. Wouldn't you like a hug?"

The gold eyes blinked, but nothing emerged from the brush.

"Okay," she said with a shrug. "Suit yourself."

Straightening, she began to walk again.

The small rustling followed her.

She paused again. This time, without looking, she said, "Are you sure you wouldn't like to come out for a hug?"

Nothing happened. No rustle or movement of any kind. She listened to the wind and watched the clouds while she waited.

Then amusement got the better of her. She muttered, "We've got this all wrong, haven't we? You're not another Peanut. You're a little Stinkpot."

Giving up, she looked around and located the stinkpot. The small gold eyes had found another deep shadow from which to watch her.

"It's okay, darling," she said gently to it. "You can hide for as long as you want to…. I'll be waiting whenever you want to come out. I'll always be here for you."

Turning back to her path, she continued on the trail, while the shadow followed close behind.

The air around her shifted, and she woke up to the sound of the jet's engines changing. They had begun their descent.

Hugging herself, she went over every detail of her dream.

Gold eyes! Like Dragos's! Sure, it had only been a dream, but everything she had ever dreamed about Liam had turned out to be true in some way. God, she couldn't wait for the little stinkpot to make up his—or her—mind to come out of hiding!

Sitting up, she looked around. Outside, faint streaks of light spanned the edge of the horizon. Alex had lowered the cabin lights after supper, and in the shadows, she saw that Eva had settled deep into her seat, engrossed in the contents of her e-reader.

Quentin and Aryal occupied the other couch, opposite Pia. They had curled up together, Quentin spooning Aryal from behind, his arm around the harpy's waist.

They looked so peaceful when they were asleep. Almost, dare one say, normal.

Muffling a snort, Pia indulged in a full body stretch. She had managed to sleep several hours, which was very good news. While she wasn't as rested as she would be if she had slept in her bed at home, she felt like she had gotten enough rest to get through the day with plenty of energy.

Her thigh itched, and absently she scratched it. She had panicked when she had begun to itch after her first shot of the protocol, but Dr. Medina had assured her it was just the drug beginning to wear off. As long as she could tolerate the irritation for the twenty-four hours or so, she was still good, still on track.

She put a hand over her stomach and whispered,

"Because you're staying right where you belong, no matter what. Little Stinkpot."

With that, she stood, collected her overnight bag and went to the back of the plane to shower and prepare for her day. She dressed casually, in a long, dark blue maxi dress, sandals, and a sheer, lightweight sweater, and took time with her makeup. While this was supposed to be an informal visit, from what she knew about the Light Fae Queen, Tatiana was relentlessly elegant, so she wanted to look nice.

When she stepped out, Eva was ready and waiting to shower too. Then Quentin and Aryal stirred and took their turns, and then Daniel stepped out of the cockpit to serve them a quick continental breakfast. After that, there was nothing left for Pia to do but watch out of a plane window and get more nervous about the upcoming week.

Tatiana was not just relentlessly elegant. She was relentlessly inquisitive as well, and in D.C. she had asked uncomfortable questions about Pia's real nature. Pia wasn't looking forward to the next week, which was all the more reason to rip that Band-Aid off and get it over with. Otherwise the trip would have been hanging over her head, perhaps for months. Now, at least, they could get on with their lives soon enough.

On Monday, to be precise.

So while she was unenthusiastic, she was certainly composed enough when the plane touched down.

Hey, baby, Dragos said in her head.

When she heard his dark, Powerful mental voice,

surprised pleasure flowed through her. *Hey yourself. How did you get here so quickly? No wait, never mind—I'm not supposed to know that.*

She could hear the smile in his voice as he asked, *Did you get any sleep?*

I sure did. Covering her mouth, she yawned. *I missed you, though. How did your night go?*

I went fishing and flew up around Big Sur, he said. *It was good, but I missed you too.*

She confessed, *I dreamed about the little stinkpot.*

The little stinkpot? He laughed. *How did it manage to get that nickname?*

In my dream, I was hiking, and Stinkpot was hiding in some underbrush. Sharing the small story with Dragos had her grinning all over again. *In the dream, it had gold eyes like yours, but that's all I could see. I tried to coax it out for a hug, but it still doesn't want to come out and say hi yet.*

It will when it's ready.

Yes, I know it will.

As they talked, the plane taxied down the runaway to an eventual stop. *Okay,* Dragos said. *I don't want to distract you. I just wanted to let you know I was in town.*

I'm glad you did, she said. *Talk to you later?*

Absolutely. Just call whenever you have any time to yourself, and I'll hear.

Without ceremony, the jet's built-in airstairs were deployed. Quentin and Aryal descended first, and Pia followed, with Eva staying guard at her back.

As she stepped out of the hull of the plane, she paused at the top of the stairs to take in the scene.

The morning was cloudless, bright and already warm. On the east lay the San Gabriel Mountains, and at the edge of the western horizon, blue water sparkled in the sun. As they had chosen a private airstrip for landing, there was a minimum of bustle around the edges of the wide, open area.

Several Porsche SUVs waited nearby, and ten armed Light Fae guard spread out in a semicircle nearby, broadly circling a tall blond woman with short, curly hair. All eleven wore the signature tan and blue uniforms, and the woman was also armed.

Quentin said in her head, *That's a lot of guards for an informal meetup, especially when they knew you would have your own security with you.*

Is that why you and Aryal are hesitating? Pia replied. *Look how they're watching the surrounding area. They're guarding the woman—is that one of Tatiana's daughters?*

Yes, that's the younger daughter. Bailey, I think her name is.

As they hesitated, the blond woman strode forward to the bottom of the airstairs, looking up at Pia.

She said to Quentin, *Let's go.*

After a moment, Quentin said, *Okay. But I want to know why they think they need to have so many guards—either to meet us or to guard Bailey—in the heart of their own demesne.*

Oy vey. With so many watching her, she would not roll her eyes.

She muttered in Quentin's head, *If you're going to poke your nose around and ask questions, fine, just be sure to be discreet about it.*

Of course, he said, giving her a quick glance over one

broad shoulder. *I am nothing like my mate. Well, at least about discretion.*

She laughed. That was true enough. She had known Quentin for several years. He was one of the most secretive people she knew, and he had been long before he had become a sentinel and Pia had worked for him at his bar, Elfie's.

With that, she stepped down the stairs, toward the tall blond woman, who held out a hand. "Good morning, Lady Cuelebre," the woman said with a smile. "We haven't met yet, but my name is Bailey—I'm Tatiana's youngest daughter. Welcome to the Light Fae demesne."

"Thank you," Pia said, taking her hand.

While Bailey's smile had vanished quickly, she looked friendly enough. Like her older twin, the Light Fae heir and actress Melisande Aindris, Baily had thick, tawny curling hair, but unlike her famous sister, she wore hers short and tousled. Her eyes were more hazel than green, but her gaze was clear and direct, and she had a strong, firm handshake.

Then Pia almost stumbled with a lie, but she managed to catch herself before she said, *It's nice to be here.* Instead, she said, "It's nice to meet you."

"And you as well." Bailey nodded a greeting to Pia's guards, tucked her hands behind her back and inclined her head toward the waiting motorcade. "If you'd like to come this way, please."

"Certainly." Pia accompanied her to the appropriate Porsche, climbed inside with Eva, and with that, her week's visit officially began.

Chapter Four

ONCE THE JET had taken off safely, Dragos had turned his attention to making his own journey.

As fast as he might be able to fly, he couldn't beat the jet to California. If he chose to stay in dragon form for the trip, he wouldn't arrive until the evening of the next day.

There wasn't a thing wrong with that decision, and he almost chose to do it. The long, solitary flight did sound appealing. Having to relate to so many different creatures on a daily basis was wearing, and if he didn't get regular time to fly alone, he grew short-tempered and snappish. Well, more snappish than usual.

On a whim, more than anything else, he decided on a different mode of travel and called the Djinn Soren to give him a quick trip. Traveling Djinn style meant that he could get to California hours before Pia. He could still enjoy a long flight and plenty of solitude, and also be ready and waiting when her plane landed.

Sometimes it was very handy to have a Djinn owe you a favor. A few weeks previously, Soren had asked Dragos if he had any information about an upcoming commercial venture between the Nightkind and the witches' demesne. It just so happened that Dragos had developed an extensive file on the subject, and he had given a copy of the file to Soren in return for a favor. All he had to do was request the trip.

Dragos's face and form were too distinctive, so instead of booking a stay at a luxury hotel in the city, he chose a modest, remote motel bordering the nearby Angeles National Forest. After Soren had dropped Dragos and his luggage off, he checked in quickly, threw his travel bag on the bed and left again to shapeshift and take to the night sky.

Dragos didn't care for L.A.—although he had laid claim to New York long ago for tactical, political and business reasons, he wasn't fond of any city and only tolerated them at best—but he did appreciate southern California's balmy climate. The salty breeze off the ocean was the perfect combination of warm and refreshing.

By the light of a half moon, the dragon stretched out his wings and coasted on the thermals. He wore his cloaking spell to prevent detection, and after a few hours, he felt relaxed and tension free. He flew offshore some distance and dove into the water, fishing until he had eaten his fill. Then he gained altitude again and winged north to watch the ocean waves break against the cliffs of Big Sur, relishing the solitude and the clear, brilliant starlit night.

He had circled back around in a leisurely fashion, arriving at the airstrip in plenty of time to watch the arrival of the Light Fae motorcade.

Tatiana had a few formidable magic users in her

court. One of them was the captain of her guard, Shane Mac Cartheigh, so Dragos made sure to be circling very high in the air over the site and cloaking his presence tightly, as the troops poured out of the vehicles.

The dragon's sharp gaze could pick up small prey from two miles away. He had no trouble picking out the individual soldiers. He saw Tatiana's daughter Bailey direct the troops with a wide sweep of her arm. They jogged to every end of the airstrip and studied the surrounding countryside, weapons ready.

He approved of their security measures, but why was Bailey directing Light Fae troops instead of Shane? Last he heard, she didn't live in California but resided somewhere rather remote. Puerto Rico, or maybe Jamaica. She and Sebastian Hale ran a security company. Hale was Wyr and an excellent fighter, and Dragos made sure to track excellent Wyr fighters who weren't his own.

No wait, Hale had mated and retired. Bailey ran the security company alone now. So why was she here?

After thoroughly searching the perimeter, the troops down below converged again around Bailey. A few moments later, the Cuelebre jet came into view. Watching approvingly as the jet touched down in a textbook perfect landing, Dragos chatted with Pia until the jet's airstairs were deployed. Then Quentin and Aryal appeared, began to descend and froze halfway down the stairs.

They sensed something too. What did they sense?

He said in Aryal's head, *What is it?*

The harpy didn't evidence any surprise at his presence. She said tersely, *Quentin and I think it seems like a lot of troops for a simple pickup.*

It is. He told her about watching them spread out and search the area around the airstrip. *A group of that size was able to establish a secure perimeter very quickly.*

From the distance, he saw the harpy shrug. *That's probably it. Private airstrips don't have the kind of security that airports do. They were being thorough and efficient before we arrived.*

Probably, he agreed. *We do tend to be paranoid.*

Just because you're paranoid, blah blah blah, etc., Aryal told him sourly.

I wondered where Shane was, and why Bailey is here, he said. *She usually lives in Jamaica. Or Puerto Rico. Whichever one it is.*

You're so nitpicky, Aryal told him. *Now I'm wondering that too. Maybe he's on vacation. Does Tatiana's captain take vacations?*

The dragon snorted. *I have no damn idea.*

Aryal said to him, *Pia says to go ahead. What say you?*

We are *being nitpicky*, he told her. *So go ahead, but keep a watchful eye out. Report back to me if you notice anything unusual.*

You got it.

The foursome continued to the tarmac, merged with the Light Fae troops, and was swallowed up by the motorcade.

Dragos followed the motorcade until it reached the outskirts of Bel Air, the affluent neighborhood where the Light Fae Queen's residence was located. When the car carrying Pia turned onto Tatiana's street, his eyes narrowed at the barricade that waiting troops moved into place across the street. After putting the barrier into place, the troops stood at attention behind it, facing outward.

The Light Fae Queen's residence was in the same neighborhood as those of celebrities, musicians and movie stars. Ronald Reagan had once lived in Bel Air, and so had Alfred Hitchcock. Tour buses traveling through the neighborhood were a normal way of life.

As far as he knew, blocking the neighborhood off was something new. It looked as though Tatiana was taking no chances with the Lord of the Wyr's mate, an attitude that he approved most heartily.

He had watched and waited, and touched base with Pia, and indulged in paranoia. Now, there was nothing more for him to do but bide his time until he could talk to her again.

He had packed his laptop. He could go back to the motel to work. Or he could just take time off. It was rare for him to have free time on his hands. He could go fishing again, and fly over the coast and spend the week avoiding other people, and while he liked the sound of that quite a bit, his nitpicking, paranoid discussion with Aryal left him restless and uneasy.

He contacted Aryal again. *Have you arrived yet?*

Yes, we're here, the harpy told him. *Nobody's gone insane and stabbed all of us yet. Pia's in the guest suite unpacking, and we've got the suite next to hers. Tatiana is in a meeting, but she's supposed to have breakfast with Pia soon.*

What happened to the Light Fae troops in the motorcade?

They went wherever Light Fae troops go when they fly back to the home hive. They sort of dissipated and soaked into the woodwork, no doubt on the Queen Bee's orders. Aryal sounded cheerful. *But maybe they'll still swarm back and stab us all to death, before any of us can yell to you for help. You never know.*

He snorted. *Your sense of humor can be damn odd at times.*

All I'm really saying is, maybe this time, our paranoia really was just paranoia. Of all his sentinels, Aryal was the most prone to impatience, but she didn't sound impatient now. She sounded kind. *For now, everything seems fine.*

He told her, *Good enough. Report back later.*

Will do.

He had drifted south and east while they talked, over the Bel Air Country Club. Abruptly, he made up his mind, chose a direction and flew for it. While the distance would take a half an hour or so to drive by car, or even twice that, depending on traffic, he covered his trajectory within a few minutes.

When he came to Rodeo Drive, he waited for a lull in the traffic. He didn't have to wait long—traffic was unusually sparse for such a popular area. Then he dropped down and shapeshifted as he landed. Still cloaking tightly, he strolled down one of the most luxurious shopping districts in the world until he reached Van Cleef & Arpels. After admiring the jewels in the showcase, he strolled down the street to the next jewelry store.

He stopped at a few other jewelry stores, admired Cartier's display, then he came to a uniquely Elder Races jewelry store named Songs of Fire.

He had only intended to window-shop, until he laid

eyes on the firebird.

It was a necklace, very high-end jewelry, the kind of showpiece that would sell very rarely and only to a relatively select clientele. After just a brief glance, he knew the cost must be in the high six figures, if not seven.

The body of the bird rested at the hollow of the mannequin's throat. Made of fiery diamonds and rubies, it was easily as long as his thumb. The bird's eye was an emerald the size of his thumbnail. The wings swept up on either side of the mannequin's neck, tapering off gracefully so that the tips came together at the nape.

He loved having Pia as his mate for many reasons. She was sexy, and funny, and smart and wise, and far kinder than he. She curbed his worst impulses, as much as he would let her, and having sex with her was so smoking hot, they burned up the air around them when they coupled.

And one of the things the dragon loved best was to buy his mate jewelry.

Because she was his.

So when he gave her jewels to wear, they were his as well. All his, forever.

He loved to fuck her when she was wearing diamonds and nothing else. She was jaw-droppingly gorgeous when she wore jewels, all lush and naked, delicately pink in all the most private places, and sparkling bright. Pia was the crown jewel in the dragon's hoard.

He struggled with his impulses, briefly, while part of

him knew it had been a foregone conclusion as soon as he had laid eyes on the firebird.

After a moment, glancing left and right, he waited until passersby on the street were either walking or looking away. Then he let his cloaking fall away, opened the door and walked inside.

It was barely after ten o'clock, so the store had just opened for the day, and he was the only customer.

Good. He liked it that way.

As a tall, model-slim woman hurried into the store from the back, he said, "I would like for you to lock your doors while I'm here. As I plan on making at least one significant purchase, it will be worth your while."

The woman was Light Fae and beautiful, with long, thoroughbred bones, skillful makeup and designer clothes. She also looked tense and unhappy. "I'm sorry, it's against company policy to lock the doors during store hours."

Dragos paused. It was highly unusual for people to tell him no, and it was never an experience he appreciated. Cocking his head, he drew his brows together and asked, "Do you realize who I am?"

The woman looked at him, "Should I? Oh ... oh, wait. Are you Lord Cuelebre?"

"Yes, I am, and I'm here *in private* shopping for my wife." He narrowed his eyes on her. "I expect you to be discreet about my presence here."

"Sure, of course," she said, waving a hand in dismissal of the subject. "We're always discreet."

Again, he had to pause. He was a jewelry store's wet

dream. Managers bolted out of hiding to fawn over him. They had involved and passionate discussions about clarity and cut, quality grades and light.

This woman's preoccupied attitude was not normal.

He persisted. "And you'll lock the door while I'm here?"

"Oh yes, of course." She stepped around the end of one counter to walk toward the door and lock it. As she did so, she sighed. "What is it you would like to see?"

His short amount of patience was evaporating rapidly.

"I wanted to examine the firebird necklace you have on display," he told her, his tone short. "Along with the accessory pieces, but is this a bad time?"

"Excuse me?"

For the first time since he had entered the shop, she looked at him directly. He noted the shadows under her eyes. The whites of her eyes were bloodshot. His attention snagged by the small details, he took a step forward and caught a whiff of her scent.

She was not merely preoccupied and unhappy. She was quite distressed.

He sighed. The dragon didn't care if the woman was having a bad day. All he wanted to do was ignore her, examine the necklace more closely and make a buy decision.

Actually, what he would have liked to do was just steal the damn thing and be done with it, but he had started out in a leisurely, aboveboard fashion, and now the store's security system would have a record of his presence. And security recordings in jewelry stores were never stored on site, not with so many potential and extremely talented thieves scattered throughout the Elder Races.

In social situations like this, he had taken to asking himself WWPD? (What Would Pia Do?)

They had such different reactions to most things, and she was so much better at interacting and relating to people than he was, that he had learned asking himself WWPD helped avoid unpleasantness from time to time when he was in pursuit of something that he wanted.

The small exercise helped. Often, he wasn't able to achieve what Pia would *actually* do, because it was just too foreign to his nature. But more often than not, he was able to approximate something between what she would do and what was his natural inclination to do.

As a result, a rumor had started in his corporation that marriage and mating might be softening 'him up. Curious and coldly amused, he tracked the rumor down to its source, and the whispers died a quick and decisive death.

He was a contented dragon, not a tame one.

In this instance, if Pia were here, she would ask after the woman's well-being. He didn't want to go that far, but perhaps he might talk to a manager and have a normal discussion about jewelry after all.

He said, "You're clearly not focused on your work. No doubt you have some personal matter that needs your attention. Just get your manager for me, then you can take care of whatever it is you need to take care of."

The woman burst into tears.

Oh fuck. He almost threw up his hands and walked out. Only the memory of the firebird's sparkle anchored him in place.

"I'm s-sorry, there's no one else here," she said. "Two other people, including my m-manager, were supposed to show up for work, but they haven't yet. And I'm so sorry and embarrassed to burst into tears at you like this, Lord Cuelebre."

He closed his eyes briefly then told her, "Clearly this isn't the best time for you to be dealing with customers. I'll leave now and come back when your manager is available." Pausing, he stared at her. She was busy wringing her hands, while tears streamed down her face. Gritting his teeth, he demanded, "Are you paying attention to anything that I'm saying to you right now?"

"I know, I'm sorry. I a-p-p-pologize, but I've had a sleepless night. I was looking for my mother everywhere, and nobody's around, and nobody showed up for work either, even when I tried to call in and take a sick day, and …"

His short amount of patience snapped.

Staring into her brimming gaze, he said in a quiet, compelling voice, "Stop this meltdown immediately. You're calming down now. You're growing quite calm, do you understand? And lucid. You are definitely growing more lucid."

"But you don't understand," she sobbed. *There's nobody around.*"

Hm. Sometimes, when the subject was overwrought

like this, it took his beguilement a little while to take effect. Plus, there was always the possibility that she was delusional. It was very difficult to beguile a delusional person until he actually understood what they were delusional about.

"What do you mean, there's nobody around?" he asked. Beguilement also didn't work very well when he let his own impatience get in the way and upset people, so he tried to curb the sharpness of his tone. "Of course there are people around. There are cars and people in the street right now. You're growing calm and lucid now, remember? In fact, you're feeling so calm, you're quite capable of using your keys to go get that necklace for me to examine."

Abruptly, she did calm down. Her sobbing stopped as if a switch had been thrown, and her twisting hands loosened.

"There aren't any people in my neighborhood," she whispered. "My mom lives on the next block. She's gone too. We always have breakfast together, but she wasn't there when I let myself in. When I called the police and told them my mother was missing, they said they would drive by her house to check into it, and get back to me. I haven't heard from them either."

Okay. He had tried his hardest not to engage, but that snagged him. He repeated, "There are no people at all in your neighborhood."

Mutely she shook her head.

Perhaps this was the delusion he needed to under-stand to make his beguilement effective. Crossing his arms, he frowned. "How do you know this?"

"Because I live there!" the woman cried. "I know!"

Abruptly, he decided he'd had more than enough of talking to her. He snapped, "What's your address?"

Jumping at the sharp command in his voice, she blurted out an address.

He held out one hand. "Give me the keys."

The woman hesitated, then started shaking her head. "I-I don't think I c-can do tha—"

Oh for the love of all the gods. Injecting all his strength into his voice, he told her, "SHUT UP AND GIVE ME THE GODDAMN KEYS."

Her hand jerked out, offering the set to him. Taking the ring, he rifled through them until he found the right key to unlock the display case. Scooping up the firebird necklace, a matching bracelet and dangling earrings, he gave them a brief, very thorough look.

The workmanship was top-notch. He was looking forward to examining the pieces in greater depth, but for now, he shoved the jewelry into the front pocket of his jeans. He told the woman, "Tell your boss to bill me."

She stood frozen and mute, staring at him with huge eyes.

Because he had, in fact, told her to shut up. Well, that would wear off soon enough, but thank the gods, not while he was around.

Slapping her keys on the counter, he let himself out of Crazy Town and into the welcome fresh, sunlit air. Rotating first one shoulder, then the other, he angled his head and looked up and down the street.

Yes, there were people around, both shoppers walking down the sidewalks and people driving by in cars.

He was just about to dismiss the woman forever as a mental case, when one small detail caught his attention.

Everyone walking down the street was human. There weren't any of the Elder Races in sight.

That happened quite often, actually. There were far more humans than people of the Elder Races. ... But he was standing in front of a popular Elder Races shop, which strengthened the likelihood that he would see a member of the Elder Races—any of the Elder Races— quite a bit.

Frowning again, he turned his attention to the cars passing by. The next five vehicles were filled with humans too.

It was probably just a huge, boring coincidence. But Tatiana had guards barricading her street. And it *had* seemed like she had sent a large number of troops to meet Pia's flight.

Fuck it. He would go check out Basket Case's address and determine for himself whether or not there was anybody around.

When he consulted Google Maps briefly on his smartphone, he found Basket Case lived in a neighborhood north and to the west. Pulling his cloaking tightly around him, he shapeshifted and took to the air. By car, he guessed it would take Basket Case a good forty-five minutes to drive into work. Sometimes he pitied wingless creatures.

As he flew the distance, he turned over various

thoughts in his mind like searching for the spark of jewels in a mound of earth.

People, any kind of people, tended to congregate in enclaves and cluster in clumps. Sure, there were crossovers, but overall, families liked to flock to family-oriented amusements and neighborhoods. Hipsters flocked to whatever hipsters liked to do. Dragos was acres and miles and continents away from being a hipster, so he had no real understanding of that new subset of society, but he thought it involved drinking lots of artisanal coffee and organic wines.

Those who were religious behaved in the same way. They went to church, or synagogues, or temples, and enjoyed social outings together. The Elder Races also followed the same behavioral trend. They tended to shop at Elder Races stores and live in neighborhoods filled with Elder Races creatures.

The Light Fae were no exception. As a people, they tended to be clannish anyway, and Basket Case had said her mother lived on the next block over from her. It stood to reason that Basket Case probably lived in a neighborhood filled with Light Fae.

Her mother was missing. Her co-workers and manager, who were in all probability Light Fae as well, had not come in to work.

Locating the street on which Basket Case lived, he coasted down the length of it until he reached her block. Then he landed, shapeshifted and walked down the middle of the tree-lined street until he came up to her address.

It looked like a modest, smart neighborhood, with a mix of single-family homes and other houses that appeared to be divided into apartments. Along with oaks and other varieties of trees, palm trees dotted either side of the streets. Fences were painted; lawns were well kept. While modest, this was not a neighborhood in decline.

No cars traveled down the street to disrupt the direction of Dragos's stroll.

Nobody mowed their lawn.

He began to listen closely for any signs of movement in the houses he passed. There were none. A couple of houses stood with their front doors open. Silence beat down on his head, along with the strength of the southern California sun.

Basket Case had not been delusional, after all. There were no people in her neighborhood.

Some people might think that meant he owed her an apology. In fact, if he considered WWPD, she would definitely say that he did, but as far as he was concerned, it was a moot point, as he had no intention of ever speaking to or seeing Basket Case again. There was just so much of the rest of his life to live, which took a far greater urgency.

Wait, there was a sound. It came from some distance away, perhaps a couple of blocks over to the right. It sounded metallic, like a trash can had been knocked over.

He broke into an easy jog, reached the end of the block and turned right. The small sound of his own footsteps overrode what he had heard, so he had to stop once or twice to listen again before moving forward.

There—more sounds came from down this street. It was virtually a replica of the street he had just left. This was all part of the same neighborhood.

On his left, a house stood with its front door open. He passed several more houses with open doors.

Who leaves their door open when they leave their house? People evacuating, or in a panic, except how could Basket Case live in this neighborhood and not be aware of an evacuation or a panic? Had she gone out the evening before, so she wasn't home to notice this general air of abandonment?

His mind shot to the unpleasant heart of the matter. Was he really going to have to talk to her again, after all?

There. He stopped.

The noises came from behind that stucco house. Now that he was closer, it sounded louder, like there were several creatures making it. A pack of dogs, perhaps, rooting through an alleyway. If people had left in a hurry, some of them might have abandoned their pets.

He walked around the side of the house. A six-foot-high privacy fence surrounded the backyard, so in the last several feet, he gathered up speed and leaped over it.

The backyard was charming and as well kept as the rest of the neighborhood. He jogged to the back fence, gathered himself and leaped again.

As he landed in the alley, he startled a group of people.

Quite a large group of people, all Light Fae, in various modes of dress. To a one, they were streaked with blood and open wounds.

Staring, he straightened from his landing crouch as the group whipped around to glare at him. Their eyes were all black. No whites.

Some had only half their faces, the remaining flesh looking as though it had been chewed by wild beasts.

People tend to flock, and these were no exception either. Moving as one, they hurtled at him. They were incredibly, impossibly fast. There wasn't enough room in the alley for him to shapeshift and launch. Then he thought to turn and leap back over the fence.

As he crouched to spring, the foremost of the group gathered into a huge leap and landed on his back, knocking him off balance. It was followed by two more. Then the entire group was upon him. Pain flared as one of them bit him on his arm, tearing through the skin.

Like the snick of a trigger on a gun, Dragos's mind clicked over to Plan B:

Fight savagely and throw lots and lots of fire.

He cut loose.

Chapter Five

TATIANA'S RESIDENCE REMINDED Pia of classic old Hollywood grandeur. The white mansion had Corinthian-style columns in the front, large receiving rooms and a large pool in the backyard surrounded by an immaculately kept garden.

The furnishings inside were classic old-world Hollywood too. Pia's suite had a massive four-poster bed in the bedroom with a peach coverlet and sheer drapes tied back, and antique Chippendale furniture. She had a sitting room all to herself, with a wood fireplace and two divans, and her bathroom had a walk-in, marble bathtub with gold furnishings.

After unpacking and admiring the view out her windows, she texted Eva. I'm ready to go downstairs.

Within the next breath, a rap sounded on her door. Eva didn't wait for a reply but opened it and stuck her head in. "I'm ready too."

Unless they encountered a situation that warranted a change in plans, for now, while Pia was in the Light Fae Queen's residence, she would have one guard with her at all times, so that Quentin, Aryal, and Eva could rotate shifts around the clock.

Pia hoped that would help to generate a relaxed atmosphere among everyone, and besides, the other two were close by if anything happened.

She stepped out in the hall and took the stairs with Eva by her side. Just like earlier at the airstrip, Bailey had evidently been waiting for them, and she moved smoothly to the bottom of the stairs to meet them.

At least Bailey wasn't flanked by ten more guards inside the house, Pia thought wryly. Because that would be awkward.

"Are you all settled in?" Bailey asked.

"Yes, thanks," Pia replied cheerfully. "The place is magnificent. Is it all right if we look around?"

"Sure," Bailey told her. "I'll come with you."

"Are you my babysitter?" Pia asked, smiling.

The Light Fae woman returned her smile, but like before, on the tarmac, it was brief and faded again quickly. "It's my pleasure to spend time with you."

So she is *my babysitter,* Pia said to Eva. *I don't mind. I suspected there would be somebody, but I did at least expect some kind of greeting from Tatiana when I arrived.*

Guess a Queen's gotta do what a Queen's gotta do. Eva's mental voice sounded dubious.

Pia, who had been on the receiving end of many events that needed immediate attention, didn't feel nearly as dubious about Tatiana's absence. Things happened, and when you were a demesne leader (or his mate), sometimes you had to react quickly.

Bailey turned to indicate the direction of the rear of the house, and as they fell into step beside her, she said,

"My mother asked me to apologize for her. She had planned to be free to greet you personally, but in the last two days she's been dealing with an unexpected situation. I'm sure you know how it goes."

"I do, actually," Pia replied. "We're often disturbed in the middle of the night for one reason or another. Demesne business never seems to stop."

"I get it," said Bailey. They reached double French doors, which she opened. She led them onto a wide verandah. "You and Dragos are one of those places where the buck stops, aren't you?"

"Yes, we are."

"My mom is too. It's one of the reasons why I mostly live somewhere else. I love my family, but I don't want to eat, drink and sleep all things Light Fae. And I *really* didn't want to go into the family business. I have about as much acting ability as a tin can."

"What do you do, at your home?" Pia asked her curiously.

Her first impression of Bailey had been one of tough competence, but the other woman hadn't seemed all that friendly during the motorcade ride to Bel Air.

Now, she received a different impression. Once they stepped inside the Queen's home, Bailey seemed to have relaxed, and as a result, she had grown more talkative.

"I run a security company out of Jamaica," Bailey said.

"What does a security company do?" Pia asked.

"It can involve anything from supplying bodyguards for specific events to either running expeditions or providing security for them. One of the most interesting expeditions we recently undertook was to retrieve a magical library from a deserted island."

"You're talking about Carling Severan's library, aren't you?" Pia said, her attention snagged by the scenario. "I heard about that. It must have been a fascinating trip."

"Yeah, it was. That was the trip my business partner Sebastian found the love of his life, mated and retired." Bailey gave her a sidelong grin. "But usually things aren't quite so eventful. On a daily basis, my job mostly involves a lot of drinking and suntanning. When we take on jobs to pay the bills, it can often involve a lot of fighting too, so by and large that makes me happy. Only thing I don't like is the paperwork. Sebastian, my former partner, used to take care of most of that, but now that he's retired, I've been drowning in it."

Out of the corner of her eye, Pia saw Eva smile. Pia told Bailey, "My husband hates paperwork too, which is why he has several assistants."

"Yeah, assistants." Bailey heaved a sigh. "If you don't do it yourself, you have to be a manager for somebody else who does. Or even a couple of somebody elses. I'm just not sure running a business by myself is going to work out. It takes away from the drinking and the suntanning."

Pia laughed. "Bummer."

As they talked, they stepped outside to walk the grounds. In the growing heat of the sunny morning, Bailey unbuttoned the jacket of her uniform, shrugged out of it and slung it over one shoulder. Underneath she wore a shoulder harness and gun over a plain white, short-sleeved shirt. The shirt hugged her lean torso and supple, muscled biceps.

Pia had gotten used to the sight of armed people as a daily occurrence a long time ago, but she couldn't help but wonder—if Bailey was comfortable enough in her role to shed the uniform, why did she still feel the need to go armed?

After all, Bailey was essentially in her own home, and there were other guards around. When sentinels or other military personnel visited Pia and Dragos's house for any length of time, they disarmed, left their weapons in a safe place—usually Dragos's office—and relaxed. It was only when they were making a brief stop that they didn't bother.

Did Bailey stay armed because Pia and her three guards were here? Or was it some other kind of Light Fae protocol? If Bailey was supposed to be on duty, perhaps she was required to be armed at all times.

And if she ran a security company in Jamaica, what was she doing here in southern California?

Pia filed those questions away to pursue another time. Hopefully, everybody would relax during her visit, and she might find a time to ask some of them at a later date.

The grounds were beautifully landscaped. They weren't as glorious as the former Elven High Lord's consort Beluvial's grounds were, but Beluvial had a special gift for growing things.

Still, the Light Fae Queen's gardens were beautifully

kept and worthy of being featured in *Home & Garden*. When Pia thought of the sturdy, no-nonsense landscaping of grass, mulch and trees that they had decided to do around their home in upstate New York, a pang of homesickness washed over her.

Thrusting that aside, she focused on the present. "The weather is gorgeous," she said, taking a deep breath and turning in a circle to admire the cloudless blue sky. "When I left home last night, we were getting a combination of rain and snow, with a forecast of more snow through today."

"Did you bring your swimsuit?" Bailey asked. "L.A.'s forecast for the next week is more weather like today's."

"I didn't think to pack it," she confessed.

"No problem. Mom keeps a variety of swimsuits for guests, or if you want, we can always send out for one." Bailey had taken them on a big circle around the property, and as they turned to stroll back in the direction they had come, she added, "Sorry, I'm not as good at hostessing as my sister Melly or my mom. I should have asked you if you've eaten breakfast already."

"How is your sister doing?" she asked. Earlier that year, Melly had been kidnapped and held hostage by a ruthless Vampyre elder. In the process of being rescued, Melly and the Nightkind King, Julian, had rekindled an old love affair.

For some reason, Pia's question made Bailey's expression darken. "We don't talk like we used to, but she seems well, and she sounds happy."

Bailey didn't appear to appreciate her sister's rekindled relationship. It was time to move the conversation on to something else.

Pia told her, "I'm glad to hear it. It was a terrible thing that happened to her. And thank you for bringing up breakfast. We had a light breakfast on the plane, but I wouldn't turn away a second chance to eat."

The shadow passed from Bailey's expression, and she gave Pia a quick grin. "We'll be like Hobbits then, and eat second breakfast. And elevenses too, if you'd like."

Pia laughed. She liked Bailey. "That sounds good."

As they neared the house, a tall, elegant Light Fae woman stepped outside and strode toward them.

Tatiana, the Light Fae Queen, had finally freed herself of other obligations and was coming to greet Pia.

Pia took in the other woman's appearance. When she had seen Tatiana at political functions, the Light Fae Queen had worn haute couture. She had the height, the beauty and the poise to carry off outstanding creations.

Now, the other woman wore black clothes and boots. The shirt was tailored, and the cut of the pants elegant, and if those boots cost under $5,000, Pia would eat her own sandals, but still, the outfit was much more plain than any she had previously seen Tatiana wear.

Instead of sporting a mop of curling dark blond hair like her daughters, which was typical for the Light Fae, Tatiana must have had her hair straightened, for it fell like a sleek waterfall to below her shoulder blades.

Her expression was poised and serious, and in the full, bright light of the sun, faint shadows darkened the skin underneath her eyes. The last time Pia had talked with her, Tatiana had been smilingly inquisitive, poking at Pia delicately like a cat batting her with a paw. Tatiana's claws had been sheathed at the time, but you knew she had them.

Something's wrong, Pia thought. She let the observation sit in the back of her mind, while internally, she braced herself.

"Good morning," Tatiana said as they came up to each other. "Bailey tells me that you had a good flight."

"Yes, we did," Pia said. Then, because she sometimes had claws of her own, she batted gently at the Light Fae Queen. "Thank you for sending such a robust greeting party."

Was that a flicker of response in those famous, beautiful green eyes?

"You're welcome," Tatiana replied. "We take the issue of your safety while you visit here very seriously. Please, come sit with me on the verandah. Bailey, would you see that refreshments are served?"

"Certainly. Pia and I were discussing doing just that."

Pia told Eva, "Why don't you go with Bailey?"

"Sure," Eva said. Telepathically, she asked, *You've got your phone?*

Yes, in my pocket. I can text if I need you.

Bailey inclined her head to Pia, and she and Eva strode into the house.

Pia followed Tatiana to a white painted, wrought iron table and chairs that were tucked well into the shade of the porch roof. As they seated themselves, she told the older woman, "Your home is lovely."

"Thank you," Tatiana replied. "I've lived here since the early twentieth century, when moving pictures were just becoming all the rage. Perhaps sometime you might be interested in touring the Northern Lights Studios. We've kept a great deal of memorabilia, and it can be amusing to take the tour."

At last, something that Pia could answer with complete honesty. "I would love that," she said, even while she noted Tatiana's use of words.

"Sometime," the Queen had said, not "this week." Was she beginning to let Quentin and Aryal's paranoia infect her?

"In the meantime," Tatiana said with a smile, "Bailey and I have been talking about possibilities for your visit. We wondered if you would enjoy staying at Melly's beach house in Malibu. The beach is quite lovely, and the swimming and surfing is very nice at this time of year. The house is located in a gated community, and after what happened to Melly earlier this year, the security has been increased until the area is all but airtight. It's a wonderful vacation spot. I've stayed there myself from time to time."

But I'm not on vacation, Pia thought.

She watched Tatiana closely, but the other woman had many years of experience with being in the limelight, and her poise remained flawless.

Still, the suggestion said everything. Something *was* wrong.

It was oh, so tempting to accept the invitation. She could soak up some sun, get in some pleasure reading, and swim to her heart's content, and probably even sneak in a few conjugal visits with Dragos.

But if word got out that this was how she spent much of her week with the Light Fae, what would the other demesne leaders think? How would the human government react?

She chose her response with care. "What a wonderful suggestion. Thank you for thinking of it, but I thought the point of this week was that you and I interact and get to know each other a little better? If I stayed at the Malibu beach house, I'm concerned that the other demesnes and the White House administration will not look on that choice with favor. And I have too many commitments over the next several months to consider committing to another week's visit."

The Queen was not pleased. Pia watched the subtle tightening of Tatiana's mouth. "Yes, I know." Tatiana snapped off the ends of the words with a delicate bite. "You made that clear when I emailed you and suggested that you visit at a later date."

Despite the diversity among the Elder Races, there was one thing demesne leaders had in common that Pia had noticed over the course of the last eighteen months—absolutely none of them liked being crossed or denied in any way.

Well, Tatiana was just going to have to suck it. Pia didn't like the situation any more than the other woman did, and her time and needs were just as important as anybody else's.

Still, if something was indeed wrong, she didn't want

to make a bad situation worse. Again, she chose her words with care.

In a quiet, nonconfrontational voice, she said, "I know the terms of the diplomatic pact are difficult, and not just for all the demesne leaders but for their families as well. The last thing I want to do is disrupt your life as much as mine has been disrupted by this. If there's anything I can do to help ease the situation for you, please let me know. I'm happy to help you in any way I can."

The Queen stared at her with hard, glittering eyes just long enough to make Pia nervous. After all, she didn't know Tatiana well, but from everything she had heard, the other woman was formidable in every way. This exchange wasn't going to lead to some sort of royal tantrum, was it?

Then Tatiana let out an explosive sigh and rubbed her eyes. "Just tell me this much," she said. Her words were still clipped and short, but there seemed to be slightly less bite to them than before. "Did Dragos follow you here?"

Pia froze. In retrospect, she should have expected something like this, but she hadn't and the bald question caught her completely flat-footed. Like a frightened rabbit, for a moment she didn't even breathe.

Trying to stall for time, so she could think of a good way to lie, she asked cautiously, "Why would you ask such a thing?"

Tatiana barked out an unamused laugh. "Pia, everybody in the entire world has heard in great detail what happened when you went to visit the Elves in South Carolina."

"Yes, but the Wyr and the Light Fae aren't enemies, like we were with the Elves when that happened," Pia said cagily, while telepathically, she said to Dragos, *Uh-oh, I think we've been made.*

I'm busy dealing with an unexpected issue, he said tersely. *I'll be in touch soon.*

What on earth was he busy with?

She had just time to turn grouchy at his response when Tatiana snapped, "Stop prevaricating. I've asked you a straight question, and I expect an honest answer. Is Dragos here in Los Angeles or not?"

Great, numbskull. Just bloody great. You've already managed to piss off the Queen. What's next on your agenda, setting fire to Disneyland?

"He might be," Pia muttered. Nerves had taken her over. She scratched at her itchy thigh then smoothed the fabric of her dress over her thighs with tense fingers. "Nobody said he couldn't take a vacation in southern California during my visit."

Inexplicably, Tatiana relaxed. Sitting back in her chair, she said, "This visit of yours might turn out to be useful after all. Why don't you get in touch with him and ask him to come here, will you?"

She felt her eyebrows shoot up. "You—*want* him to come here?"

The other woman snorted. "You probably don't hear that all too often."

"No, frankly, I don't. I love my husband very much,

but I'm under no illusion about how stressful his presence can sometimes be to others." She hesitated.

The strength and range of Dragos's telepathy was a closely guarded secret. Not only that, but he had sounded pretty terse when she had telepathized to him earlier, so under Tatiana's watchful gaze, she pulled out her phone to text him.

Tatiana knows you're in L.A., and she's asked you to come here to her residence. After a moment's thought, she added, I think there's something wrong.

Just then Bailey stepped outside again, along with Eva. Behind them, a Light Fae servant wheeled out a cart filled with a variety of food and drink.

Tatiana said to Bailey, "Stay and join us."

With a quick questioning glance at Pia, Bailey replied readily enough, "Sure."

As she pulled out a chair and sat, Pia glanced at Eva uncertainly. As Tatiana's daughter, Bailey had many liberties that others wouldn't necessarily be expected to share.

If they were at home, Pia would invite Eva to sit down with them too, but while the Wyr had many complexities that other cultures did not—such as the intricacies and dangers in mating, and the tensions that lay between herbivores and predators—in many ways they had a less formal society than other demesnes. To the Light Fae Queen, Eva was a servant and a guard, but to Pia, Eva was also a friend.

Oh, screw it.

She looked at Tatiana. "Eva is a friend of mine. If I

were at home, I would invite her to join us too. Would that be acceptable to you?"

The other woman's eyebrows rose, but despite the tensions just a few moments ago, she replied easily enough, "I have relationships like that as well. As you might remember from your aborted dinner party, my Captain Shane is one of them. As long as you count her in your inner circle and you give her access to privileged information, she can join us."

That was better. Feeling more comfortable, she smiled and nodded to Eva, who pulled out a chair opposite Bailey and sat.

"Thank you," Pia said to Tatiana, while she glanced down with a frown at her phone. It was unlike Dragos to take this long to text her back. What was his unexpected issue? It didn't have anything to do with Liam, did it?

The server set place settings and food on the table. Bailey said, "Eva and I double-checked all the recipes to make sure everything was vegan."

That brought Pia's attention up from her phone. She glanced again at all the dishes. There were scones, fresh strawberries, a pot of something that looked like cream but Pia's nose told her was coconut cream, not dairy, little round containers that looked like avocado mousse with pretty flecks of orange zest, some kind of berry crumble, and a complex savory salad with tossed greens, olives, and other vegetables.

Usually Pia could eat one or two dishes out of an entire meal's spread, but the Light Fae had ensured that she could eat everything on this table. It was a kindness she hadn't expected.

"This was really thoughtful of you," she told them. "Thank you."

"It was no trouble," Tatiana replied. "I often choose to eat vegan meals." As they helped themselves from each dish family-style, the Queen added, "I'm afraid I don't have much time I can spare for you. That was one of the reasons why I suggested the Malibu beach house. Over the last few days, a situation has developed that is consuming a great deal of my attention and resources."

Pia and Eva exchanged a glance. Pia asked, "You said that was one of the reasons behind the invitation to enjoy the beach house. What were the other reasons?"

This time, it was Tatiana and Bailey's turn to exchange glances. She had time to note that Bailey's expression had turned closed and unrevealing. Then Tatiana gave her a direct look. The Queen's gaze had turned grim.

Tatiana said, "Your safety. If you insist on being here this week, the Malibu house is the best place for your protection."

Carefully, Eva put down her fork. Her demeanor changed from relaxed to sharp and poised. She asked, "Are you saying that you don't feel safe in your own home?"

"That is a possibility, yes," Tatiana replied. The Queen looked perfectly calm and composed as she scooped a tiny spoonful of avocado mousse out of a cup. "Naturally we're doing everything we can to counteract that."

Oh Lord, Pia muttered in Eva's head. *It looks like my travel curse is alive and working fine. I can't wait to hear what Dragos has to say about it.*

Just then, her phone coughed out a polite-sounding *ping.* Murmuring an apology, she checked the screen.

It was a text from Dragos. Damn right something's wrong. I'll be there as fast as I can.

Whatever his situation had been, it seemed to be over with. Telepathically, she accused, *How do you know something's wrong? You haven't been relaxing or fishing at all, have you?*

He didn't respond.

She was getting practiced at refraining from rolling her eyes in public. Setting her phone aside, she said, "Again, my apologies for letting the phone interrupt us. Dragos is on his way. He says he'll be here as soon as he can."

"In that case, there is no point in going over everything twice," Tatiana said. "We should finish our meals while we can."

With that ominous-sounding statement, the Queen calmly speared an olive on her fork and ate it.

Chapter Six

AFTER A SECOND'S hesitation, Pia followed suit. Between her new life as Dragos's mate and having a small child, at least for several months, in the household, she had learned to eat heartily when she could.

The quality of the food was excellent, of course, and her constant appetite ensured that she cleaned her plate.

The conversation could have turned stilted, but it didn't. Tatiana plied her with questions about her daily life and asked after Liam. Part of Pia found the chitchat rather bizarre. Clearly something was wrong enough to require Tatiana's attention, but the Queen behaved as though there was nothing more urgent than discussing school choices for children.

"Your son sounds remarkable," Tatiana said. "And how unusual that he has grown so much, so fast."

"Yes, he's remarkable in every way," Pia replied. "And while his magical nature has made him unique, the important thing is, he's a really good person. I don't just love him, I respect him."

When Tatiana met her gaze, her expression had turned warm and sympathetic. "I understand. I have always felt that way about my daughters too."

For the first time since arriving, Pia felt like she had made a real connection with the Queen. Any sense of achievement she might have felt at that was overshadowed by concern for Dragos.

When the dragon took to flight, he could eat away miles like chomping through popcorn, but it had been over half an hour since he had last texted her. Shouldn't he have arrived by now?

She resisted fiddling with her phone. It hadn't pinged with a new message, and obsessing over a phone while in someone else's company was rude. Older members of the Elder Races, for whom new technology was intrusive anyway, were especially offended by such things.

While she wasn't sure how old Tatiana was, she knew the other woman had to be quite old. The *Sebille* had been an exploratory voyage sent out by Tatiana to find new lands for her people to settle in, and that ship had wrecked off the coast of Bermuda in the fifteenth century.

When Pia saw that Eva's plate was clear, she murmured to her, "Please go update Quentin and Aryal, and let them know Dragos will be here any minute."

"Sure thing. I'll be right back." Eva stood, gave Tatiana a slight bow and left.

One moment trickled after the other, excruciatingly slow. Tatiana sipped coffee and remarked how well the daffodils bordering the verandah were doing, while Pia wanted to do nothing more than jump to her feet and pace. Bailey, clearly not immune to the slow-building tension either, rubbed her face with both hands.

Eva returned, and this time, she took a position behind Pia's chair, while she said telepathically, *They're coming down ASAP.*

Good, Pia said.

New footsteps sounded at the doorway, and a tense-looking Light Fae guard appeared. "Ma'am," he said to Tatiana, while he flicked a nervous gaze to Pia. "Lord Cuelebre has arrived and is outside."

"Don't make him wait," Tatiana said impatiently. "For the gods' sake, let him in."

The guard grew more nervous. "My apologies, ma'am, but we can't."

"What do you mean?" the Light Fae Queen snapped.

As Pia pushed to her feet, she reached out telepathically, *Dragos? What's going on?*

There was no response.

No response, yet Dragos was here.

The wrongness of that pounded in her head. Abruptly, she abandoned civility. Quickly she strode into the house, leaving the others to exclaim and scramble after her.

As she moved toward the front of the house, she picked up her pace until she was running. The double front doors stood open, framing a sunlit lawn. Two guards stood in the doorway, facing outward.

There was just enough space between the two guards. As Pia wriggled between them, she realized they both had their weapons drawn.

Had the world gone crazy?

She almost made it through to outside. Exclaiming,

both of the guards grabbed for her, and one of them managed to catch hold of her by the arm.

"Are you insane?" she hissed furiously. "Put up your weapons. We're invited guests!"

"Lady, you don't understand," the guard said. "You can't go out there."

"Like hell I can't," she said between her teeth.

She caught what happened next in snatches.

Dragos stood on the lawn, his clothing torn and bloody. He had his hands on his hips, his hard expression grim. One of his forearms had cloth tied around it.

Then Pia was knocked sidelong, as Eva tackled the guard who held on to her arm. Stumbling, she fell to the ground, scraping her elbows on the concrete pavement while Eva and the guard grappled with each other.

Bailey ordered, "Stand down! *Everybody stand down!*"

Then Quentin and Aryal shot onto the scene like dark, deadly arrows. Pia didn't catch what happened next, but as she rolled to her feet, suddenly weapons were drawn everywhere, Light Fae guards and Wyr pointing guns at each other.

Dragos roared, "WYR—LOWER YOUR GODDAMN WEAPONS *NOW!*"

Immediately, Quentin and Aryal stepped back, guns lowered. As Quentin edged around the group to approach Pia, Eva jerked out of the grasp of the Light Fae guard she was grappling with and threw a roundhouse punch at him that made him stagger.

"Don't you *ever* put your hands on her again, asshole," Eva snarled at the guard. Then she skipped back a

PIA DOES HOLLYWOOD ✧ 81

couple of steps, hands raised.

Quentin threaded between people to reach Pia, his blue eyes hard. He asked telepathically, *You okay?*

Yes. She turned and started toward Dragos again.

This time Bailey lunged forward to grab her by the arms.

"What the hell?" Pia snapped. "Will you people stop grabbing me?!"

"I'm sorry, I'm sorry, I'm sorry," Bailey said. "Pia, you can't."

Quentin rounded on Bailey and slammed a flattened hand against her chest, physically knocking her back from Pia, while Eva growled, and the whole fiasco might have escalated again, except that this time, Dragos said sharply, "Stop. *Everybody stop.* Pia, do what they say and stay back."

Exasperated now, and still badly unsettled, she wheeled around to stare at him. "I don't understand. Why can't I come close? How the hell did you get hurt?"

"I got curious and started poking around." When he met her gaze, she saw that his gold eyes had darkened. Compared to their normal brilliance, they looked almost dull.

Immaculate and as coolly poised as if she were still drinking coffee on the verandah, Tatiana stepped around the clump of angry, unsettled people on her doorstep.

The Light Fae Queen and the Lord of the Wyr regarded each other for a moment.

Dragos growled, "Your people have a discipline problem under pressure, Tatiana. Tell them to put their goddamn weapons up."

Unhurriedly, she studied him while making no move to do so. "You're infected."

"Apparently, yes," he said between his teeth. "With whatever the fuck this is."

Infected.

The word bounced around in Pia's head. This time, instead of struggling to get to him, she met Quentin's grim gaze. Her breathing sounded harsh to her own ears.

"Did you get bitten?" Tatiana asked.

"On my arm," he said tersely.

"What happened to the one who bit you?"

"It was with a group of thirty or so others. I burned them." Dragos's gaze switched to Pia. He told her, "Whatever this is, it's affecting my Power. I can't telepathize, and I can't shapeshift either. I had to hot-wire a car and drive here."

Struggling to sound calm and rational, Pia said, "What the fuck is happening?" She rounded on Tatiana. "What do you mean, he's infected?"

Regret filled Tatiana's expression, along with resolve. The Queen said to Bailey, "Call Shane back to the house. Tell him to hurry." Then she turned to her guards. "As long as Dragos remains lucid, don't shoot him."

✧   ✧   ✧

DESPITE DRAGOS'S WARNING to stay away from him, Pia plunged across the lawn. Eva, the sentinels, and Bailey followed her immediately. Uneasily, Dragos took several steps back as they neared.

"You guys have to stop," Bailey insisted. "He could turn rabid at any time."

Dragos felt the urge to bare his teeth at her, but he was mindful of the guns still trained in his—and now Pia's—direction and refrained. Tatiana's guards were spooked enough. If he showed how he was really feeling, the gods only knew who they might accidentally shoot.

"I'm not turning rabid right at the moment," he snapped.

Tatiana's guards weren't the only ones who were spooked. Bailey gave him a leery glance. She asked, "How long has it been since you got bitten?"

"Over forty minutes ago." He turned his attention to Pia, who was pacing around him in a wide circle, wearing a fierce scowl.

"We're not in California five minutes." She flung up a hand, fingers and thumb splayed. "Five minutes, Dragos, and you managed to get bitten by... by ..." She stopped pacing. "What bit you?"

"An infected Light Fae."

She studied him worriedly. "Show me the wound."

In answer, he unwrapped the cloth from his forearm and showed it to her. They both regarded the bite mark, which was clearly visible, the tears in his skin dark red.

"It's negligible," he said. "Barely more than a nuisance. It should have healed within ten minutes. Instead, it's not healing at all. After I burned the pack, I discovered I wasn't able to telepathize or shapeshift."

As he spoke, he was aware that the others were listening as well. Aryal swore softly and raked her hands through her hair, while Quentin pinched the bridge of his nose.

Bailey's eyes had widened at his story. She said, "Your constitution is very strong. The people we know who were bitten turned within fifteen or twenty minutes. This is very bad news. So far as we knew, only the Light Fae have been affected. We had no idea until now that others of the Elder Races could be infected too."

He had no intention of mentioning it to anyone, but he could feel the infection from the bite, coursing through his veins like poison, and his Power had roused to combat it. It felt strange and tiring. He was almost never too hot, but now he had broken into a light sweat and felt both hot and cold at once. Was this what a fever felt like?

Pia stood facing him with her feet planted apart, hands fisted at her sides. She looked grim and determined, and ready to do battle. "I want to telepathize with you so badly right now," she muttered.

He glanced at the others and said to her, "I want to telepathize with you too."

"It's going to have to wait," Bailey told them. "We think the contagion is passed through blood and saliva. Dragos, you're a walking hazard—you've got blood smeared all over you. We have to burn your clothes and get you as disinfected as we can."

"Privacy is the least of anybody's concerns right now," he said. "Let's do this. Somebody get me something clean to wear. How are you disinfecting people?"

"We've been using propyl alcohol, along with an antiseptic detergent." She turned away. "Follow me."

He did so, and the others trailed after him several feet behind.

Bailey led them around the far corner of the house, to an area where they had constructed a large structure draped with plastic.

"I see the tour of the grounds you gave me earlier didn't lead over in this direction," Pia said to Bailey, her voice bitter.

The other woman looked chagrined. She said to Dragos, "It's a decontamination chamber. It's pretty makeshift but it will get the job done. When you step in, leave your clothes and shoes by the outer flap. We'll get you something else to wear. You'll find the alcohol and detergent in the shower area. I'm sorry, the shower's cold—for now, we're just running water from the sprinkler system."

"A cold shower is the least of my concerns right now," he snarled. He stalked into the plastic-draped area and stripped to the skin.

Bailey was right, the construction was crude but effective. After he had stripped and left his clothes in a crumpled pile where she had indicated—saving the jewelry, which he kept in one hand—he stepped into the makeshift disinfectant chamber. He scrubbed his whole body for at least ten minutes with the sharp-smelling detergent then doused himself with the propyl alcohol, making sure to scrub and douse the jewelry as well.

Both the alcohol and detergent should have stung in the bite, but they didn't. The skin around the bite had turned numb, and he still wasn't healing. As he prodded the wound and inspected it, dark streaks had begun to shoot out from the puncture wounds. His Power might be slowing down the progress of the poison from the bite, but it wasn't stopping it.

Once he had finished showering, they had collected other medical supplies, and he securely taped a bandage over the bite mark. He even wiped off his phone thoroughly with disinfectant.

He dressed quickly in the jeans and shirt they had found for him. The gods only knew where they had found an outfit big enough for him, because typically the Light Fae were nowhere near his massive size. The clothes were snug, but they would do. Stuffing the cleaned necklace, earrings and bracelet into the pocket of his new jeans, he stepped out of the plastic area.

Pia stood nearby with the other Wyr waiting in a close, tense huddle, while the Light Fae had retreated to give them some semblance of privacy.

After sweeping the scene, Dragos kept his eyes on Pia. She was biting her nails and tapping one foot nervously. He strode over only to stop several feet away, clenching his fists in frustration. The urge to take her into his arms was almost overwhelming. He hated he couldn't act on it.

Her gaze went immediately to the white bandage on his arm. "How is it?"

"Still there," he replied. He looked at the others. "Give us some space, will you?"

Reluctantly they stepped away, Aryal scowling over

her shoulder at them.

Pia burst out, "This is so wrong. I can't even touch you."

"I know," he said, very low.

They stared at each other. The morning had evaporated into a hot afternoon. Indirect sunlight gilded the ends of her hair, and sent shafts of illumination into her dark gaze. She said between her teeth, "Everybody on the property has supersharp hearing, and I want to telepathize with you *so badly*."

He pulled out his phone. "Let's text it."

She snatched hers out of the pocket of her maxi dress, and her slender fingers flew over the tiny keyboard. When she was finished, she did one final, emphatic stab.

His phone pinged, and he looked down at the screen.

She had written: I don't have time for a meltdown. Let's pretend I just spat out a lot of AGH and UGH and OMG HOLY FUCK!!! and get it out of the way, shall we?

A hint of laughter ghosted through him. He texted back, I'm almost sorry I missed that.

She gave him a brief glare and turned her attention back to her phone. We need to get enough privacy so that I can try to heal you.

Agreed, he replied. But you might not be able to. You're taking a drug protocol that suppresses your own abilities.

For a moment she stood frozen, staring at him with wide eyes, her phone dangling from her lax hand. Then she set to typing again furiously. The dose is wearing off. I'm supposed to take the next round this evening.

"I just want you to be braced," he told her aloud, quietly. He texted the rest. You're supposed to take the dose before the effects of the protocol have fully worn off. If you wait and take it late, you could endanger both yourself and the baby.

That was assuming he could stave off the effects from the bite long enough, but he didn't text that thought. A look of sheer terror flashed across her face, and he had to clench down again on the need to take her into his arms.

Then her jaw firmed, and she said, "Let's not get trapped into thinking it's an either/or scenario. None of this may be necessary. Wait here."

"Pia—" he began.

The glare she threw at him had sufficient strength to stop him in his tracks. "I know what you're going to say, but don't even bother, because we don't have time for that either. Let's pretend we had an entire argument about it—you just said we can't, and I just said we have to. You said what about the secret, and I'm telling you right now *I don't give a fuck about the fucking secret!*"

"Calm down and think about what you're saying," he rasped.

"Well, I can't calm down, and I am thinking about it. Think about how many people already know, Dragos. The sentinels. Eva and Hugh. Liam, Dr. Medina and Dr. Shaw, and you know Stinkpot's going to know as soon as he—or she—gets big enough. And probably there are other people I'm forgetting right now. No, wait! That's right!" She threw out both hands. "Beluvial and some of the Elves know. The list keeps getting larger and larger, and chances are, we won't be able to keep a lid on this forever."

"We've got a lid on it for now," he snapped.

"Yes, but it's a train crash in slow motion. It might take months or it might take years, but sooner or later, that lid is gonna blow. In fact, the way I feel right now, I could just shout the fucking secret to the whole fucking world. So just wait there a fucking minute."

Belatedly he caught up with everything that she had said.

Stinkpot?

She had sworn more in the last three minutes than she had in the last six months, but he had gone well past the point of any desire to laugh. Crossing his arms, he glared back at her but complied. He watched as she strode over to the other Wyr. After a silent exchange with them, Quentin reached into his pocket to pull out something and hand it to her.

She swiveled and jogged back, but instead of stopping in front of him, she continued past. "Come on," she said over her shoulder as she headed back around the corner toward the decontamination chamber.

He threw a wary glance at the Light Fae by the front door. They were watching him closely. As he spun to follow Pia, he noted security cameras mounted high along the corners of the walls. He would bet all the jewelry in his pocket that he was being watched right now.

Rounding the corner of the building, he came upon

Pia, who had opened up a pocketknife. Her face tight with determination, she gestured to him. "Come on. Pull the bandage back."

"Damn it, Pia," he growled. "This isn't private either. We're being watched."

She blinked. "What do you mean?"

He jerked his head up, toward the direction of the security camera, and she rolled her eyes. She looked beyond fed up. In fact, she looked like she had joined Basket Case and driven straight to Crazy Town, and he knew if she wasn't stopped, she really would shout the fucking secret to the whole fucking world.

He needed to derail that meltdown, if he could. Glancing around, he eyed the decontamination chamber.

"Take a breath," he told her. "The camera won't be able to see anything we do behind a few layers of plastic. Come on."

It was her turn to follow him as he led the way through the thick plastic flap. Ignoring the sharp, acrid smell inside, he turned to face her.

Still wearing an expression that told him she was close to the edge of panic, she rotated her wrist at him. "Hurry up. Pull back the bandage."

"Lower your voice," he whispered. "The plastic will stop the camera from seeing what we're doing, and it might muffle our voices somewhat, but there are still a lot of people around with very sharp hearing."

"I don't care," she muttered. She gripped the knife like she meant to stab herself with it.

He roared, "I care! I mean it, Pia. Get a fucking

grip."

Freezing, she stared at him. For a moment, her mouth wobbled precariously, then she firmed up. The strain was evident in her voice as she said, "I apologize. It's just—Dragos, when I weigh the secret against the thought of possibly losing you, there's no contest."

At that, he wanted even more desperately to put his arms around her. Instead, he whispered fiercely, "One way or another, it's going to be okay. But we've got to think our way out of this. We're not going to get there if either one of us is in a panic. Understood?"

Jerkily, she nodded. "Yeah."

"Okay. Get braced. This isn't pretty." He pulled back the bandage and showed the bite wound with the slowly expanding dark streaks to her.

He watched as the sight hit her like a blow. She swallowed and blinked rapidly. "Does it hurt?"

"No," he said tersely. "It should, but it doesn't."

Giving him another terror-filled glance, she took the knife and held her hand over his forearm.

Uneasy at exposing the open wound so close to her, he muttered, "Careful, don't touch me."

"I'm not touching you!" she flared. Then, giving him an apologetic look, she said more temperately, "Just hold still."

He did, clenching his fist as she drew the pocketknife across the end of one forefinger quickly. Bright blood beaded in the cut. She squeezed her finger, forcing the blood to flow more freely until a few precious drops fell onto the open wound.

He had said they had to think their way out of this, but he couldn't help but feel they were fast running out of options. If this didn't work ... well, they would cross that bridge when they came to it.

If it did, the gods only knew how they were going to explain their odd behavior or his unexpected healing in such a way to keep the fucking secret.

Chapter Seven

TOGETHER, THEY STARED at the bite mark while Dragos waited for the signature wave of her Power to wash through him. Her healing Power was an amazing, unstoppable sensation, unlike anything he had ever experienced. When Pia healed him, he felt like he was bathed in light.

Nothing happened.

The moment dragged on, weighing down both their shoulders. Pia rubbed her forehead, and her mouth shook again. "It didn't work."

"Well, now we know," he said. He slapped the bandage back into place over the wound. "So now we've got to think about alternatives. Let's go talk to Tatiana. I want to know how this outbreak happened, why the fuck they didn't warn us, and what measures they're taking to contain it. Maybe they're close to finding some kind of effective antidote."

Straightening, she nodded. "While you were showering, Tatiana's captain arrived and went inside."

"Let's go see what they have to say for themselves."

They pushed their way out of the plastic-draped chamber and walked to the front lawn again, where

Quentin, Aryal and Eva, along with the Light Fae, were waiting.

The other Wyr joined them, questions in their eyes. Aryal's gaze dropped to the bandage Dragos still wore, and she swore, while Eva's face tightened and Quentin blew out a breath.

Together, the group of Wyr strode toward the front entrance of the house, where several guards stood. As they drew near, the guards swung around to stand in formation, and all of them had their guns trained on Dragos.

Bailey was with them. She stepped forward, her expression regretful. "I'm so sorry, Dragos," she said. "But we can't let you in the house."

"That's preposterous." Pia gestured angrily. "Look at him—he's in perfect control of himself."

"Yes, he is, for now," Bailey agreed. The Light Fae woman gave them an apologetic glance. "But that could change quickly, and if it does, we won't be able to reason with him. And even without his ability to shapeshift, your husband is still very powerful. He could do a lot of damage, and infect a lot of people, before we could stop him." She turned her attention to Quentin, Aryal and Eva. "None of us want to hurt any of you, but we may not have any choice. You may not have a choice either, and you all need to be prepared to face that fact."

Pia whitened, while Aryal rubbed her face and swore.

"She's right," Dragos said, interrupting whatever Pia might have said next. He asked Bailey, "Where are we going to meet?"

"My mother is willing to let you into the back garden," Bailey told them. "Shane will be there, and she'll be surrounded by guards, but it's a compromise of sorts, and it would allow us to discuss possible next steps."

"Fine. Let's go," Dragos said. As they strode around the house to the back, he asked, "What about the neighbors? These houses and yards are large, but that's no real protection, either for them, or for any sensitive discussions we might have."

"That's not an issue," Bailey told them. "Bel Air has already been evacuated."

Unexpected anger burned, hot and bright. He demanded, "Since when?"

"We evacuated for several blocks around 10 P.M. last evening," Bailey replied, giving him a hassled glance. "We thought at the time we were just erring on the safe side, but as it turns out, it's good we did."

"This morning, you brought my wife, and my people into this mess," he snarled. "You got me involved in this."

"Look, in the last forty-eight hours, this outbreak has grown exponentially," Bailey shot back, her eyes sparkling with quick anger. "As soon as my mother got the first hint that something might be wrong, she sent for me and tried to cancel Pia's visit, but you guys insisted. This morning we tried to remove Pia to a safe location in Malibu. And *you* aren't supposed to be anywhere near here, Lord Cuelebre, let alone wandering around and sticking your nose into things, so let's try to stop with blame throwing and work on finding some solutions, all right?"

As she spoke, she opened a gate in a stuccoed wall and strode through.

Dragos met Pia's burning gaze. Behind them, Aryal whispered, "If I start slapping people, I might not be able to stop."

"Everybody's stressed right now," Quentin muttered. "Rein it in, harpy. Don't add to it."

"Much as it pains me to say this," Dragos growled, "Bailey is right again. Arguing about what happened and who might be to blame is useless. In any case, this is no longer just a Light Fae problem, because it sure as hell has become a problem for the Wyr." He looked at Pia and said more quietly, "Come on."

At that, he reached out to put a hand at the small of her back, but then he caught himself up.

Reaction glittered overbright in Pia's eyes. Tightening her mouth, she stepped through the open gate, and he followed.

✧   ✧   ✧

PIA'S NERVES WERE jumping all over her body. She felt as if she might leap out of her own skin like a scalded cat, if given the slightest provocation.

Avoid stress, the doctor had said. Eat lots of good food and enjoy this little mysterious bun cooking in the oven. Ha!

Dragos stalked by her side, a dark lowering shadow, his hard face cut with severe lines. Even in his human form, he moved with a lethal fluidity that spoke of the fact that he was an apex predator. He was faster and stronger than anybody she knew. It was no wonder the Light Fae were still terrified of him, despite the fact that he couldn't shapeshift into the dragon.

From the short time he had disappeared to shower, his eyes had grown darker, and the dark lines shooting from the bite wound was one of the most terrifying things she had ever seen. He never got sick, never. It was as if germs vaporized whenever he became exposed to them. The fact that he wasn't healing from the bite might force her to consider a terrible choice—her mate or her child.

No. Her mind went into a frenzy, and she tore that idea to shreds. There had to be other alternatives, ways to think outside of this box that they didn't know about yet. If the Light Fae were writing off others who had been infected as a lost cause, it might be in part because they had turned so quickly. Dragos hadn't, yet. They needed to gather as much information as fast as they possibly could.

"Fight it," she said to him a low voice. "Fight as hard as you can."

Just as low, he replied, "I am."

Bailey had paused to lock the gate behind them, and as they rounded the rear corner of the house, she took the opportunity to send Dr. Medina a quick text. Urgent - How long can I safely go without taking the protocol?

When Pia had collapsed in D.C., they had put the doctor on retainer. The doctor would continue to see other patients only for minor things during the length of

Pia's pregnancy, so that meant she was able to answer almost immediately. Don't tell me you lost your dose?

Not relevant, Pia replied. Too busy to explain. How long can I hold off taking the protocol without endangering the baby?

Dragos had moved close to read over her shoulder. As she glanced up at him, he gave her an approving nod.

"They're waiting for us," Bailey said.

Dragos gave her a sharp look from under lowered brows. "We'll be there in a moment. This is urgent."

Bailey's baffled expression clearly indicated she couldn't imagine what could be more urgent than their current situation, but she subsided, while Quentin and Aryal exchanged a frowning glance. Things were too complicated to give them a quick, telepathic explanation, so Pia took the short route.

She said in Eva's head, *Please fill Quentin and Aryal in about the pregnancy and drug protocol. The protocol is suppressing my healing abilities, which we think might be why it didn't work when I tried to heal Dragos. We're trying to find out how long I can go off the protocol, without endangering the baby.*

Oh shit, Eva muttered. The glance she gave Pia brimmed with compassion. Then her expression changed. She looked like she did when she was thinking fast and hard. *Pia, what about Liam? He has some of your healing ability, right? Do you think he might be able to help Dragos?*

She recoiled, and her response came straight from her gut. *No! We would never bring him into something dangerous like this. Honestly, the thought never occurred to either of us.*

Okay, honey. It was just a thought. Eva gave her a troubled glance. Then she turned to the sentinels.

Dr. Medina's reply to Pia's question was slower in coming. Pia could almost see the doctor's cautious, thoughtful expression. As short an answer as I can give—I don't know. There are lots of factors to take into consideration. Any delay will cause a risk, and the risk will escalate the longer you go without. I wouldn't want to see you go more than two days at most, and only that long if you have no other choice. Right now, your doses overlap. As the last one wears off, you're taking the next, because the protocol takes at least eight hours to work through your system. Let me know when you're able to talk. I'll be on standby.

After typing out a quick thanks, she met Dragos's gaze. Two days, and from the sound of it, Dr. Medina didn't feel good about pushing it that far.

And that was assuming that Dragos could even hold strong against the contagion for that long. They still didn't have enough answers yet.

All Pia knew was that she wasn't letting go of anybody—not Dragos, and not the baby either. They needed to see what they could do to increase their odds.

She gave him a nod, and he said to Bailey, "We're ready now."

As they continued around the rear corner of the house, Eva slid up to Pia's side and dropped a hand onto her shoulder. Grateful for the support, she reached up to squeeze the other woman's fingers. Then Eva's hand fell away, and they reached the verandah.

The Light Fae had not been idle. Tatiana and Shane

were bent over maps that had been spread out on the wrought iron table. Several watchful guards were stationed around them.

Roughly ten feet in front of the verandah, a long line had been created with masking tape on the lawn. Shane and Tatiana straightened as Bailey and the Wyr drew near the line.

"Stop," Shane said.

Pia had met Shane for the first time at the summit in Washington. His reputation tended to precede him, as he was known as one of the Elder Races' most Powerful magic users. The Queen's captain was a tall, handsome man, with a square jaw and a ready smile, and the athletic build of a football player or a jouster. He wore his curly hair trimmed short, and carried an aura of deep, old Power that she had found appealing in D.C.

Now, that Power was roused and pointed at them like a sharpened sword.

Watching him warily, along with the several guns that the other guards pointed at them, the Wyr came to a halt. Bailey, Pia noted, stayed with them. It was a reassurance, of sorts.

Dragos put his hands on his hips. "I have to tell you, Shane. The guns are getting old. Note that my sentinels are not pointing weapons at you."

"I'm sorry," Shane said. "But none of my people are infected, either. This is very unfortunate. Right now, your people are in a hell of a lot more danger from you than they are from us."

Tatiana spoke up. "You must understand. This isn't

personal, Dragos. We are taking a significant risk by allowing you to come this close. All your people are welcome to join us." The Queen looked around the group. "In fact, we strongly urge them to. Please, come up onto the verandah. He'll slaughter all of you if and when he turns."

"We'll stay right here," Aryal said. The harpy stood with her arms crossed.

"Have it your way," Shane said briefly. "Just know you're welcome. Dragos, we need to come to an agreement. As long as you stay on the other side of that line, I'll know you're still lucid. If you cross that line, it means you no longer remember what I've just said, and I'll have no choice but to take you down. Anybody who remains on the other side of that line is going to be collateral damage."

"Understood." Dragos turned to Pia. "Go."

Did he feel the contagion growing stronger? Dread made her stomach bottom out. Fighting back panic, she said in quiet, anguished protest, "No."

He raised one hand toward her then let it fall back to his side. His darkened gaze was intent, and his hard expression had gentled. "Listen to me," he said quietly. "They're right. If I turn, then I might kill you all before they stop me. Those things I came across—they were incredibly fast. You need to get some distance from me while you can."

"Is it worse?" she whispered, searching his gaze. "Can you tell?"

His expression turned inward. "Not yet. And I am

fighting it as hard as I can. But if we separate, you can keep searching for a cure even after I've turned. If you stay by my side, it might doom us both."

"That's right." She whirled back to face Tatiana and Shane. "He might turn, but that doesn't necessarily mean he'll be lost to us if he does. We need more than a line made of masking tape. We need chains, and something to anchor them to."

Shane's eyebrows rose. He asked Dragos, "You will allow us to chain you?"

"I'll put the chain on myself," Dragos said.

Tatiana and Shane looked at each other. Shane said, "So far, I've had to destroy every infected one that I've found—they've been too dangerous and frenzied to capture. Dragos might be our best opportunity to find a cure for everybody."

"Get an SUV back here, and the heaviest chains you can find," Tatiana rapped out. With an assessing glance at Dragos, she added, "You'd better make it two SUVs."

"Ma'am," said one of the guards. "The gate to the back isn't wide enough for vehicles that big to fit through."

"I don't give a shit," she snapped. "Knock down a wall, if you have to. Move fast!"

They leaped to obey. Within short order, Pia heard an engine gunned, and a Hummer slammed through the gate opening, tearing down a good chunk of the wall with it. Roaring around the corner, it stopped between the house and the swimming pool. It was joined immediately by another Hummer.

A few minutes later, a couple of guards brought thick

ropes of chains. Pia didn't want to think about where they might have had the chains stored, or for what purpose. Working quickly, and with Dragos's active cooperation, they soon had him chained to both vehicles, a Hummer on either side of him.

Watching him test the give on one of the chains, Pia rubbed her arms and shivered. Even though it was for everybody's protection, and it might possibly save his life, the sight of him trapped between the two vehicles was terrible.

Tatiana walked up beside her, watching Dragos with a calculating expression. The Queen asked, "Do you think it will hold him if he turns?"

If Dragos had been able to shapeshift, she would have snorted a derisive laugh. As it was, she shook her head and answered honestly, "I don't know."

Tatiana sighed. "Well, we had to try. At the very least, it might slow him down."

Shane had helped with chaining Dragos, and now he moved up beside the two women. "We need to move on to business."

Dragos shook his arms to settle the chains into place. "Tell us everything you know."

Shane crossed his arms, watching him. "When we got word of the first sightings, two nights ago, we moved in fast and hard, and I thought we had eradicated the problem, but then more infected people popped up just north of here. Until you, we thought this was a purely Light Fae affliction—virtually every infected person we found was Light Fae."

"No humans?" Pia asked.

He shook his head. "Not at first. Not until today. A few hours ago, we discovered a couple of magic users who lived at the edge of a Light Fae community had turned. Most humans appear to be unaffected."

"The contagion might be sorcerous in nature," Dragos said. "I can feel it attacking my Power."

Shane paused, studying him. "That would make sense. And if it's true, most humans won't be affected at all, but all of the Elder Races, along with any humans that have sensitivity to magic, will be susceptible to it."

The other Wyr stood nearby, listening intently. Quentin interrupted. "What do you mean, that makes sense? What makes sense about it?"

Shane sighed. He looked at Tatiana. "I haven't had the chance to tell you this bit yet. When you called me in, we had just finished engaging in a skirmish with several of Isabeau's Hounds."

Who was Isabeau, and why had they killed her dogs?

As Pia looked questioningly at Tatiana, the Queen said in brief aside to her, "My twin sister. The Hounds are her attack force."

Ah. The twin sister who was also a demesne ruler, the Light Fae Queen with the Seelie Court in Great Britain, from whom Tatiana and her followers had fled in the fifteenth century. What kind of history lay between the two sisters that was so bad that, centuries later, Isabeau would send an attack force to Tatiana's demesne? Or perhaps the attack force was in response to some new antagonism?

Glancing at Dragos, she gave Tatiana a silent nod of acknowledgment as she chewed on a thumbnail.

Shane continued, "We killed several of them, but a few escaped." He paused and took a deep breath. "Tatiana, I think one of them was Morgan. I didn't get a good look at him, so I can't say for sure. If it was Morgan, he was one of the ones who got away."

For the first time since Pia had arrived, Tatiana showed a visible reaction at the news. She flinched, and the skin around her mouth whitened, while fear flashed across Bailey's face. Quentin pursed his lips and somehow managed to look both intrigued and pained at once.

Dragos asked, "Who's Morgan?"

Yeah, good question, Pia thought.

Then, in the next moment, she realized it wasn't a good question at all, as both Shane and Tatiana turned to stare at Dragos.

"What do you mean, 'Who's Morgan'?" Tatiana asked. "Isabeau's Chief Hound. He's been in her Seelie Court for centuries, remember?"

Dragos's expression tightened and briefly he closed his eyes, which was when Pia realized what a major misstep he had just made.

Slowly, his gaze as sharp as swords, Shane added, "You must have met him several times before, Dragos. You did frequent the Seelie Court decades before the rift between Tatiana and Isabeau occurred, and Morgan wasn't with her then, but at the very least you must have heard of him. Morgan of the Fae is one of the oldest, most famous sorcerers in the British Isles. Surely, you haven't forgotten—or have you?"

Dragos looked at Pia, and the frustration and self-recrimination in his darkened gaze made her want to put her arms around him so badly, she almost went and did it despite the danger of contamination. Biting her lip until it bled, she wrapped her arms around her torso and forced her feet to remain planted where she stood.

"Actually, I had forgotten," he bit out.

Tatiana took a few steps toward him. Her gaze had turned fascinated, speculative. "That's unlike you, dragon. You have always had a remarkable mind for minutiae, even centuries later, and the time you spent at the Seelie Court is no piece of minutiae."

Of all the things they had worried about—the baby's safety, Pia's fucking secret—they had forgotten to be on guard for pitfalls that might stem from Dragos's memory loss.

And of all their secrets that could have been betrayed, she thought this one would cause the least amount of damage, but still, Dragos would hate it. He hated the thought of exposing anything that might be seen as a weakness.

As he had said to her before, the dragon was one of the oldest of the Elder Races, and he was not a peaceful-minded creature. He had made enemies. Dangerous, old enemies.

Pia didn't pause to think. Instead, she leaped into the conversation. "It *is* unlike him," she said nervously. "Do you think the infection could be affecting his cognitive abilities?" Turning to face Dragos, she asked, "Dragos, do you remember anything at all about Morgan?"

Dragos's eyelids had lowered when she'd started speaking, and his expression had turned guarded and closed. Walking to the rear bumper of one of the Hummers, he leaned back against the car. The pose should have suggested relaxation. Instead, he looked as coiled as a king cobra about to strike out. Despite the heavy chains shackling his wrists and ankles, if it came down to a free-for-all melee against all the others, she would bet everything she had on him.

Much as she hated to admit it, the Light Fae were right to keep their guns trained on him, even now.

He said, "Now that you've mentioned him, of course I do. I don't recall my time at Isabeau's Court, though. And as Tatiana said, it's unlike me to forget."

Tatiana tapped a manicured finger against her bottom lip. "Maybe this is what happens to every victim before they turn. They forget who they are and become like rabid beasts. Only for them it happens quickly, within fifteen minutes or so. But Dragos is changing much more slowly. I wonder what else you might have forgotten."

Dragos's shuttered gaze met Pia's again, and then he looked away. "Once I've been healed, it won't matter, will it?"

"One hopes," Tatiana murmured. She had not lost that dangerous, speculative expression. "It would be most unfortunate if you suffer permanent memory loss from this. As long-lived as we are, it does not do to lose track of memories of dangerous things."

In retrospect, it had been rather miraculous that Aryal had been silent to date, but now she snapped, "Which is all the more reason for us to step up the pace of this conversation, don't you think? I'm growing gray hair over here. Goddamn, let's stop the useless speculation about whether or not Dragos has forgotten anything, and move along already, before he does actually have time to turn. So, Morgan might be one of the Hounds in L.A. So what?"

For once, Pia felt overwhelmed with gratitude for Aryal's abrasive, impatient nature.

Thank you, she said in Aryal's head.

You're welcome, the harpy said shortly. She hitched a shoulder. *Also, I was just being honest.*

That, Pia believed. But she still could have kissed her.

"So," Shane said, "if Morgan and others of the Queen's Hounds are here, and the contagion is sorcerous in nature, I don't think this outbreak is some terrible random act of fate. I think it's a planned attack on the Light Fae."

Bailey said suddenly, "That would explain why the outbreaks keep popping up in different places. When someone is infected, they don't really have time to travel around before they turn. This hasn't behaved in the way other diseases do. With some things, like the flu, the incubation period is long enough that someone who has been infected can travel across the world before they realize they're sick. Whereas here, if someone gets bitten, they change almost immediately. The infected haven't had time to travel to other areas."

"At least not yet," Pia said.

Silence fell over the group as everyone stared at her, absorbing the implications of that statement. Reluctantly, she continued, "This might have started with the Light Fae, but it's now jumped to both humans and to the Wyr. What if other races react to the contagion more slowly, like Dragos has?"

Quentin rubbed his scarred, handsome face with one hand and muttered, "If that happens, then this could go global very quickly."

Shane said crisply, "We can't let it go global. That's all there is to it."

"Then we need two things, as fast as we can get them," Tatiana said. "We need to stop the Hounds from spreading this further, and we need a cure."

"Actually, we need three things," Bailey said. "We not only need some kind of cure. We need an inoculation, so that further outbreaks can't happen. That's the only way to completely neutralize whatever this is."

"I know which part is my fight," Shane said. "I need to go."

"Quentin and Aryal will go with you," Dragos told him. "Because this is now our fight too."

Pia burst out, "Before they leave, I need to talk to all of you. Quentin, Aryal, Eva—come over here to Dragos." She looked at Tatiana. "I'm sorry, but this is confidential. Can you and your guards give us some space?"

The speculative expression flashed through Tatiana's gaze again, but the Queen replied, "Of course. Everyone, fall back to the verandah."

"Don't take long," Shane told them. He had turned grim, his ready smile nowhere in evidence. "We need to stop the Hounds before they can do more damage."

Pia stepped directly in front of Dragos, her back to the verandah. As Eva, Quentin and Aryal gathered around her, she gestured wordlessly to Dragos to step around the end of the Hummer.

Eyes narrowed, he tried, but the chains wouldn't let him move all the way to the far side of the vehicle.

So be it. She whispered to the others, "Cover what I'm doing."

With a smooth, liquid glide, Quentin stepped into place behind her, and Eva and Aryal crowded close. When she pulled out the pocketknife, Dragos covered his mouth with one hand and growled softly, "There are at least half a dozen guards watching us right now."

She whispered furiously, "We're going to keep trying this every hour on the hour if we have to, until we find some other alternative that works. Every hour that passes means I have that much less of the drug in my system." She looked sidelong at Aryal. "Are you guys blocking their cameras?"

Aryal studied the area, eyes narrowed. "Yeah. I really think we are."

Pia told Dragos, "Now stick your damn arm out."

Running his sharp gaze over the tableau, he complied, and peeled back the bandage. Pia stared at the bite wound worriedly.

Had the dark streaks grown? Did it look the same as it had before? Honestly, she just couldn't tell.

With a quick slice, she cut the end of her thumb and let the blood drip over the torn skin. Collectively, the five of them stared at the wound for several moments. It was such a small wound to mean so much. As Dragos said, it should have been negligible at most.

It couldn't take everything away from her.

Pia wouldn't let it.

Chapter Eight

E VA AND ARYAL'S eyes had gone wide—neither one
of them had witnessed Pia heal anyone firsthand.
Behind her, Quentin had stopped breathing.

Nothing happened. The bite mark remained, the
puncture wounds raw.

Without a word, Dragos smoothed the bandage back
into place.

"Damn," Aryal breathed.

Snapping the knife closed, Pia jammed it back into
her pocket. She told Dragos, "This is our life now. Every
hour, on the hour. I'm not even scheduled to take the
injection until this evening. And we'll count every hour
past then."

He nodded. "We'll figure out a way to hide it. Until
we have another alternative."

"That's our cue to get out of here," Aryal said to
Quentin. She paused "Just how worried should I be
about coming up against this old, famous Morgan of the
Fae?"

Quentin said without hesitation, "He's going to kick
our asses."

The harpy barked out a short laugh. She had

switched over to fighting mode, Pia saw, and looked fierce and eager. "So be it."

The pair strode for the verandah where Shane waited. When they left, Bailey went with them.

"You go on too," Pia said to Eva. "Give us a minute."

Eva paused with a frown. Telepathically, she said, *Okay, but for the record, I don't like leaving you so close to him right now.*

Duly noted, Pia told her. *And, for the record, if he changes, I'm faster than you are.*

Yeah. Okay, you have a point, Eva said. *Just—Pia, you might be faster than I am, but that doesn't mean you're going to react fast if Dragos changes.*

Pia reached for patience. Eva was only trying to protect her. *I appreciate your point, but I'm still asking you to go.*

Emitting a soft growl, the other woman complied.

Pia turned back to Dragos, cupping her elbows so that she didn't forget and reach out to him. "We touch each other a lot," she muttered. "I'm always just about to reach out to you, and then I have to catch myself up."

"I know," he said. "I'm doing the same. It's driving me insane." With a quick, impatient flick, he snapped the heavy chain that shackled one wrist. "I'm also beginning to realize how much I pace."

"We'll get you free." She tightened her fingers, gripping herself hard. "Dragos, Eva brought up Liam. She wondered if he might be able to help you."

His darkened gaze flared. "No! We're not going to bring him into this mess."

She jerked her head in a nod. "I had the same reaction. I could never knowingly put him in danger." She searched his expression. "But what if we're wrong? Your life could be at stake. Hell, mine and Stinkpot's could be too."

He shook his head, stubborn determination stamped on his rugged features. "We're not there yet. Did you notice? The wound hasn't gotten worse."

Her breath left her, and she sagged. "I wasn't sure. I didn't dare to hope."

"I noted before—the ends of the streaks were just beginning to show at the edges of the bandage." He held out his muscled forearm for her to inspect. "Look. They haven't gotten worse. We're holding our own."

She sagged. "That's the best news I've gotten all day."

"Chin up." Dragos's voice had gentled. "Look at me."

She lifted her gaze to his. He looked so wrong, with his fierce gold eyes darkened. It was like the sky going dark in the middle of the day. The sight made the tiny hairs on the back of her neck raise.

But his expression was all his, fierce and tender at once. Giving her a slight smile, he whispered, "I'm putting my hand to your cheek right now."

The stubborn strength that had kept her knees locked threatened to give way. Closing her eyes, she whispered back, "I'm putting my arms around you, and leaning my head on your shoulder."

"And I'm stroking your hair, and kissing you." He

took a deep breath. "And I am always, always going to hold on to you with all of my strength. Always, Pia."

The adamant surety in his voice steadied her like nothing else could have. Following his lead, she breathed deeply, taking in the reality of him. Then she looked up at him again. "We'll deal with whatever may happen next."

His smile deepened, and she knew that he had gone back to the first time she had said it. "We always do," he agreed. "Now, since I'm chained up here, and Quentin and Aryal have left, why don't you go take a look at those maps and see how many areas this contagion has spread to?"

"Okay." She nodded. "We need to know that. If it spreads too much further, they're going to have to go public about this. I guess I can understand why they haven't yet, but this might have grown into something they can't control anymore."

"If they continue to be reluctant to go public," Dragos said, "then we will. I hate as much as anybody the fact that this appears to be yet another catastrophe instigated by the Elder Races, but people need to be aware of the danger. Too many lives are at stake. If there's any political fallout from this, we'll just have to deal with it later."

"Understood," she said. She searched his expression. "Do you need anything—anything to drink or eat?"

"I'm good."

"I'll be back soon." She smiled and whispered, "I'm kissing you right now."

He swore softly, frustration evident in the snap of his voice. "I'm kissing you too."

With that she had to be content enough to walk away.

✧ ✧ ✧

WWPD WAS NOT the only question Dragos asked himself. Sometimes he asked, What Would Pia Think? (WWPT?)

That question never failed to entertain him, because as smart as he was, and as good as he was at playing chess, he could never guess her thoughts with 100 percent accuracy. He imagined he could play the small mental game throughout the endless centuries like puzzling over an eternal Rubik's Cube. He knew there had to be a magical combination that would unlock the entire puzzle, but he suspected he would always be doomed to failure.

Because they were polar opposites in so many ways. He was a predator; she was an herbivore. He was intensely male, and she was all woman. Often they didn't laugh at the same jokes. Really, it was amazing they got along as well as they did. Sexual attraction helped, but it couldn't be the entire glue for the relationship.

Somehow, magically, they clicked. She gave when he couldn't—and he was honest enough to admit that she did it more often than he did. And when she couldn't, he found a way to reach for her.

As he watched her walk away, he knew they had just experienced another point in time where their views divided, and he wasn't even sure if she had been aware of it.

What he had said was true: too many lives were potentially at risk from this contagion. When she had agreed, he knew she had leaped to concern for all those who might be in danger, but he hadn't.

People died all the time. They always had, and he cared about almost none of them. The dragon was not generous with squandering his emotions.

No, his concern about the increasing number of lives that might be endangered was strictly limited to two things. One was, how much danger did it mean for those few people the dragon did care about?

The second was, the more people who died from this, the worse the political fallout would be. Last month, the human world had put the Elder Races on notice—they were watching, and they were disturbed by what they saw.

In fifty short years, the spring massacre in the Nightkind demesne, along with all the other issues that had arisen over the last eighteen months, would become nothing more than minor footnotes in history. But right now, the massacre was too soon, too raw in people's memories.

This problem in the Light Fae demesne might not be Tatiana's fault, but the humans wouldn't see it that way. Non-magical humans might not be susceptible to catching the contagion, but they could be caught and killed by hordes of those who had turned. This was everybody's problem, and it appeared to have been caused by the Elder Races. It wouldn't matter to the human government that the Elder Races demesne responsible lay in Great Britain. When reacting with racial bias, people tended to get very simplistic in their thinking.

So aside from the personal considerations, the calculator in Dragos's head clicked on, and he looked at this whole fiasco as a numbers thing. The more people who died or were victimized, the larger the fallout would be, and right now, he couldn't finish that equation, because they hadn't succeeded in containing the hazard yet.

He needed to step up the preliminary work with the Dark Fae engineers he had hired from Niniane, just in case. The Other land under his control from upstate New York was a massive, protected place, but it was also almost completely pristine and undeveloped. The political and social tensions from the summit in Washington D.C. had shown that co-existence might not remain a safe option for the Wyr, and he was determined that they would have a safe place to retreat to, if it ever became necessary.

Retrieving his phone from one pocket, he sent a few texts. As he hit send on the last one, out of the corner of his eye, he watched Tatiana walk toward him.

It was a maneuver he did not appreciate, as the Light Fae guards with their guns perpetually trained on him grew tense.

Crossing his arms, he leaned back against the Hummer's bumper and tried to appear relaxed. As Tatiana drew near, he said, "I'm still not thrilled with how trigger-happy your guards look, Tatiana. If you need to have a conversation, are you sure you wouldn't rather call me on my cell?"

Tatiana did not look over her shoulder at her guards. "They won't shoot unless you present a clear danger to me."

Then they were stupid for not shooting him right away, because the dragon always presented some kind of danger.

But so often it didn't do to educate people out of their stupid.

He crossed one booted foot over the other, basking in the hot sunlight, while he waited for the Light Fae Queen to get around to whatever it was she wanted to talk to him about.

"How are you holding up?" she asked.

That wasn't what she wanted to talk about. He said in a brief, flat reply, "I'm fine. How are you, Tatiana?"

He could tell by the flicker in her eyes and the tightening of her mouth that she hadn't liked the sarcasm in that. But she chose to answer him honestly. "I'm pretty much as you might expect. My people are being decimated, so I'm enraged and worried." She hesitated. "Would you consent to letting my doctors draw some of your blood? We need to find out everything we can about the contagion in order to stop it."

He didn't like that, and his knee-jerk reaction was to refuse the request. You could learn a lot by studying someone's blood, and it was never a good idea to give anybody information about himself.

As she watched his face, she urged quietly, "Please, Dragos. You're the only person we have so far who might provide clues about how to build a resistance against the contagion. Everyone else has succumbed in less than half an hour."

Goddammit. He rubbed his forehead, struggling with conflicting impulses. Finally, he said, "The only way I'll let you have samples of my blood is if we get a doctor that I trust into your labs to monitor what you do with it. And I want the samples destroyed afterward."

"Damn it, Dragos, this isn't the time—" she began.

Impatiently, he interrupted her, "I mean it, Tatiana. Like the guns you have trained on me right now—my decision isn't personal. But you know as well as I do that Powerful spells can be built on someone's blood. I'm not letting go of something that could be that valuable and dangerous to me without putting some guarantees and protections in place beforehand."

Biting her lip, she nodded after a moment. "Okay, you have a point. It's a deal. But what I was going to say is, the problem is how long it might take for you to get one of your doctors here. We need your blood samples now, not tomorrow. We actually needed them yesterday."

He had already squandered the trip he had bargained for from Soren, so he told her. "That isn't my problem. That's yours. You're resourceful. I know you can make it happen, if you put your mind to it."

Her expression darkened. They both knew that in order to make it happen, she herself would have to strike a bargain with a Djinn. But damned if he would incur a Djinn debt just so that he could safely give her some of his blood.

As her silence grew prolonged, he remarked, "You know, I would much rather prefer to have my own doctors study my blood and give any synthesized results or antidote to the Light Fae, anyway. If you would prefer."

"Fine," she snapped. "Which doctor do you want present?"

The two doctors he trusted the most were Dr. Shaw and Dr. Medina. Both were privy to sensitive information. Dr. Shaw was the sentinels' surgeon, and she had also consulted with him over his head injury, so she would keep any findings confidential.

But Dr. Medina was Pia's doctor, and there was no better time or opportunity to send for her than this. She could be close at hand, if they needed to prolong Pia's next injection. This could work to their advantage.

He glanced over to the verandah, where Pia and Bailey talked as they looked over the maps. He told Tatiana, "Collect Dr. Medina, along with my sentinel Grym. Grym can watch over Medina and your doctors, to make sure the lab stays secure. He'll also see that the samples are destroyed when they should be. I'll call them now to make sure they're ready."

Tatiana gestured an abrupt assent and strode back to her house, while Dragos quickly called Dr. Medina and Grym to tell them to prepare for an unexpected trip and assignment. The sentinel picked up on the second ring.

He told Grym, "A Djinn will be arriving momentarily to pick you and Dr. Medina up and bring you to the Light Fae demesne. When you get here, be sure to talk to Pia and Eva to get fully briefed on what's happening."

"What about you?" Grym asked.

"I'm not available for private conversations at the moment."

"Okay. You got it."

He hung up and punched Dr. Medina's number.

"How's Pia doing?" the doctor asked, when he spoke to her.

He glanced at the nearby Light Fae on the verandah. "I'm not able to talk freely right now. You'll find out when you get here."

"Okay." The doctor sounded uneasy. "Just tell me this much. Do I need to bring an extra dose of the protocol?"

"No," he said, and hung up.

Curious about which Djinn Tatiana would call to bargain with, he watched as a tornado of Power whirled into the yard and coalesced into a tall, feminine form. The Djinn had vaguely familiar, regal features, white skin, bloodred hair that fell past her shoulders, and the signature starlike Djinn eyes.

After the Light Fae Queen and the Djinn had a brief, private conversation in silence, the woman whirled away to return a few moments later with Grym and Dr. Medina. Both of them looked around as they got their bearings and stared at Dragos, chained to the Hummers. They converged upon Pia. Eva joined them, and the four

Wyr engaged in an intense, silent conversation, glancing in Dragos's direction often.

He composed himself to patience by closing his eyes and pretending to lie in wait in the warm sunshine during a hunt. He could wait for hours or even days for the right moment to strike at a particular prey, and had done so before, many times.

He was perfectly aware when Grym and Medina approached, but even so, Medina cleared her throat when they drew near. As he opened his eyes again, they both sucked in a breath. Medina looked frightened, while Grym looked … well, grim.

"We need to collect vials of your blood," Medina told him. She carried two bags, a medical bag and another white one with a biohazard sign on the side, which she set on the ground in front of her. "None of the Light Fae want to come close enough to do it."

"Bastards," he said without heat. His bandaged arm itched, and he rubbed at it.

Wait. His attention snapped to high alert.

His bandaged arm itched. It had gone numb before.

He wore off the bandage to stare at the wound. The dark streaks were still present, and so was the bite mark itself, but … he compared the dark streaks to the size of the bandage.

The streaks were smaller. They were definitely smaller.

He raised his voice. "Pia!"

From the verandah, her head snapped up and she bounded toward him, moving across the lawn like a bright shooting star, with Eva in fast pursuit.

Pia skidded to a halt beside the others, followed a scant moment later by Eva. Pia's gaze had gone wide with dread. "What happened?"

"My arm itched," he told her. "Look—the wound is still there, but the streaks have shrunk."

Fierce joy flashed across her face, and eagerly she reached out to hug him.

Eva grabbed Pia's arm, and he jerked back. He said, "No, not yet. The punctures haven't closed over. It's still an open wound."

"Sorry," Pia muttered, looking crestfallen. "I forgot again."

"Hold still," Dr. Medina told him, as she opened up the medical bag at her feet, snapped on a pair of surgical gloves and prepared a needle along with several empty vials. She drew six vials of blood, stacking them carefully in the biohazard bag. "Okay, we're done."

"Don't let those vials out of your sight," he told Medina and Grym. They both nodded and hurried back toward the waiting Light Fae.

As he started to smooth the bandage back into place, Pia told him, "Keep that arm out. We're not quite done. Another hour's gone by, or near enough to it that it doesn't matter."

He watched her dig out the pocketknife, glance around and nick her finger quickly. He muttered, "You're getting a little too blasé about doing that while we're under such high scrutiny."

"Not blasé," she whispered. "I've made my choice

about the risk, and now it's time to live with it."

In some ways, she could be as ruthless as any predator. Eva shadowed her actions, keeping a wary eye on the others as Pia let a few drops of her blood fall on the bite mark. As they waited, nothing appeared to happen.

Finally, Pia whispered, "We just don't know if it's working or not. It could be working very slowly, or you might be fighting off the contagion all on your own."

He smoothed the bandage back into place. "Let's agree on something right now. As long as I'm doing better, you're going to take the protocol this evening."

She scowled at him. "Dragos, we don't know why you're doing better. What if you appear to be healing, but you're not, and you get worse again? If I take that injection, my system will be suppressed for another two weeks. There's no way around that. Meanwhile, you could worsen and turn, and there wouldn't be a damn thing I could do to stop it."

She was right, but that didn't mean he had to like it. Frowning fiercely, he snapped, "Pia, we're going to have to take some steps on our best information at the time."

"I know we are!" She hunched her shoulders. "I'm just not ready to roll those dice yet. Anyway, it's not yet evening—"

"What on earth are you two arguing about?" Tatiana asked.

Dragos's head came up. Pia snapped the knife shut and jammed it into the pocket of her dress, while chagrin flared on Eva's face as she whipped around. The three of them had been so engrossed in what they were doing, they forgot to watch for anyone approaching.

They had too many dangerous secrets, but of all the secrets they carried, there was one they could throw out to appease the nosy Queen's curiosity. Without a second's hesitation, Dragos sacrificed it as a deflecting tactic.

He told Tatiana bluntly, "Pia's pregnant. We haven't decided when we're going to go public about that yet—all we knew was that we were going to wait until sometime after she got back from this trip."

Tatiana's eyes widened. Her expression, as she glanced at Pia, was filled with both wonder and compassion. "Congratulations," she said. "That's amazing news. You must be thrilled."

"Mostly, yes. We are." Pia rubbed her face. "Except now this has happened."

"You mustn't give up hope," Tatiana told her. "Dragos has made it this far without turning. That's not just significant. It's unique. If we can figure out how and replicate it, it could save a lot of people's lives."

"Yes." Pia's gaze met his. She smiled. "I have a lot of hope."

"Come into the house with me," Tatiana said. "It's been hours since you last ate something. And it's been just as long, if not longer since Dragos ate something." She told him directly, "You may not feel hungry, but you should try to eat anyway. I'll have someone bring out a tray for you."

He blew out a sharp sigh. "Fine. Thank you." Then, as Pia lingered, he told her, "Go. I'll feel better if you eat something."

She gave him a look that said she knew very well he was managing her, but when Tatiana put a hand on her shoulder, she acquiesced.

He watched until the three women stepped into the house.

Just for shits and giggles, he tried to reach out telepathically to Aryal. *How is the search for the Hounds going?*

No response. But then he hadn't really expected one. While he might be healing, he wasn't healed yet.

Sometimes when Wyr were injured, they healed faster when they were able to shapeshift, so he reached as hard as he could for his Wyr form. He knew it was there, like he knew his own shadow, but no matter how he strained, he couldn't quite reach it.

Not yet, at any rate, but he would keep trying. The receding streaks on his arm were all the incentive he needed.

He settled back against the Hummer, closed his eyes and reached for more patience. It came more easily as he thought of Morgan of the Fae, and the predator in him realized, it might not be time for him personally to hunt, but it would be again, someday soon.

Chapter Nine

THE INTERIOR OF the house was noticeably cooler than outside, where the heat of the afternoon had taken over. Pia lifted the bodice of her dress up to let the cooler air lick against her overheated skin.

"Is there anything in particular that you would like to eat?" Tatiana asked. "Or is there anything special that you need?"

Suddenly, she was ravenous again. "I feel like I could plant my face in a plate full of carbohydrates."

"Certainly." She flagged down an attendant and ordered food for them, and more for Dragos. Then she led Pia into a large, comfortable family room, where French doors looked out over the backyard.

When Eva hesitated at the door, Pia said to her, "Please wait here."

Eva nodded and eased the doors shut behind them, giving Pia and Tatiana some privacy.

Now that Pia could see Dragos again, she was able to relax.

Tatiana looked out at Dragos too, with a dubious expression. "Is he all right out there in the sun? I can have guards put up a pavilion for him."

"He's quite comfortable. Unlike me, he could bask all day in the sun." Pia chose a comfortable armchair where she could easily keep Dragos in sight and settled into it. She was too unsettled and distracted to search for the small, subtle shadow deep inside, but that didn't stop her from resting her hand protectively against the flat of her stomach.

Evening was still a few hours away. They were still within their safe zone, and she had at least three more times, maybe four, when she could try without risk to heal Dragos.

Time to take a breath. Time to try to relax. She had been in several tense situations before where a safety margin of four hours would have felt miraculous.

How would Liam and the Stinkpot get along? The thought almost made her smile.

As Tatiana settled on the nearby couch, Pia said, "I can't imagine how you must feel, knowing your sister might be trying to kill you."

In the softer interior light, the Queen's composed expression seemed to sag. "There is no 'might' to it," Tatiana said softly. "Isabeau has already tried many times in the past."

Pia bit her lip, pressing her fingers harder against her abdomen. Please gods, both her children would love each other. "She's your twin, isn't she? Did you ever get along?"

"We had a more cordial relationship once, long ago when we were children," the other woman replied. She pinched the bridge of her nose. "Although we always had something of an edge that lay between us, and we were prone to quarreling. She was jealous of privileges that I got. I'm younger than her by just a few minutes, you see, but those few minutes dictated the course of our lives. She was the heir, and I was not. I had more freedoms, and she did not. She has an aptitude for magic, and while I have force of will, I have very little else."

The space of a few years between siblings was not quite a few minutes. Already Liam seemed so much older than little Stinkpot, but that gap would close rapidly after Stinkpot was born. The gap in their ages would certainly seem negligible in forty or fifty years, very like a few minutes.

Make note to self, Pia thought. Don't play favorites with privileges.

Tatiana continued, "As we grew older, both our parents were killed in a fire. Isabeau became Queen of the Seelie Court, and that's when her jealous side took over. Eventually she changed so much, she acted like she hated me. Court became a place I avoided as much as possible, but since I was then the heir, I couldn't avoid it entirely. I never really felt threatened, though, until we both fell in love with the same man."

"Uh-oh," Pia whispered, completely drawn into the recounting of the other woman's memories. "What happened?"

"He chose me." Tatiana gave her a wry, bittersweet smile. "We tried to keep it secret for a while, but ultimately that didn't work out very well for us. I became pregnant with Bailey and Melisande, and I reached that inevitable place where I was having difficulty hiding the pregnancy. Dain—that was his name, Dain—and I had started to discuss whether or not we should leave the Court, but we hadn't made any final decision, when he was killed."

Pia sucked in a breath. She had known that, clearly, something had happened to Tatiana's lover, either a quarrel or a tragedy, because to her knowledge, the Light Fae Queen had never been married. Hearing the details seemed to bring the long-ago tragedy much closer.

She murmured, "He died when you were pregnant."

The wry, distant expression in Tatiana's gaze iced over. "Dain was murdered while I was pregnant," she corrected. "He was struck by an arrow while out hunting with his men. At the time, I was very much younger and a lot more foolish. And of course, I was also heartbroken and beside myself. I remember feeling like I had somehow left my body. I confronted Isabeau, and I didn't wait to do it until we were alone. I confronted her in front of others. It was a foolhardy thing to do, but ultimately, that probably ended up saving my life. That was the first time—at least I think it was the first time—that Isabeau tried to kill me."

"How horrible," Pia whispered.

A soft tap came at the door, and a servant poked his head into the room. "Ma'am, your meal is ready to be served," he told her.

"We'll take it in here, Evan," Tatiana replied. "It's quiet and private in here." She said to Pia, "I assume that is all right with you?"

Outside, a Light Fae guard carried a laden tray to Dragos. She turned her attention away from the window, nodding quickly. "Yes, thank you."

Tatiana didn't resume her story again until their food had been set on the tables near their seats. The Queen had a simple sandwich, while Pia had a fragrant bowl of pasta with spinach and what smelled like pieces of vegan sausage in a creamy coconut milk base. A cocktail of sparkling water and fresh juice accompanied the meal. She fell on the food like she hadn't eaten in a week.

Tatiana watched her eat with a small smile. "As long ago as my own pregnancy has been, I still remember those days of being utterly ravenous."

"Sometimes my stomach feels so empty, I feel like it's fused to my backbone," Pia muttered. She sipped at the delicious cocktail. It tasted of apricots, oranges and mint. "Please, do go on."

With a shrug, the other woman picked at her sandwich, shredding bits of lettuce around the edges. "There isn't too much more to tell, I'm afraid. The scene was like something out of a Greek tragedy, or a modern soap opera. There was even a dramatic thunderstorm that evening. Isabeau completely lost it. We screamed terrible things at each other. She accused me of stealing away her man, which was frankly delusional, because Dain was completely faithful to me. She accused me of other things as well, trying to steal her throne, and her people, and she said traitors who acted against her deserved to be killed. By being with me, Dain had sealed his own fate."

Pia stared. "So she actually admitted she killed him."

"Yes. If Shane had not been present, the spell she threw at me would have killed me instantly. As it was, he acted very quickly and deflected it."

"He has quite a reputation as a magic user," Pia remarked.

Tatiana smiled. "He did then too, and Dain had been one of his closest friends. Between Shane and Isabeau, magic flew everywhere. They literally brought the halls down around our ears. This all happened before Isabeau acquired Morgan and her other Hounds, or Shane very well might have been overpowered and we all would have died that night. I remember being shocked at the magical battle, because she had grown unbelievably strong—much stronger than I or anybody else had realized." After shredding the lettuce, Tatiana began to crumble bread between her fingers. "That night caused a schism between our people. Some stayed loyal to her, and others followed me and Shane. We were refugees for several months, traveling across Britain and building a temporary encampment along the shore until we finally decided upon sailing as far west as we could. We ended up settling here in southern California." The Queen gave her a sidelong smile. "Of course, I compressed several years into a few sentences. The actual living of the tale took much longer."

"You sent out the *Sebille* before you set sail yourself," Pia said.

"Yes, I did," Tatiana replied. "Good friends were on

that ship. We were heartbroken when it disappeared without a trace."

"Do you think Isabeau had anything to do with it sinking?"

"Sometimes I wonder if she did, although that's mere speculation. Storms happen. Ships sink. At any rate, as I said, the night of the confrontation was, I think, the first time Isabeau tried to kill me, but it wasn't the last. Every so often, an assassin shows up here, or someone tries to plant a bomb. Apparently, my sister is not just delusional, but she's unable to forgive or move on with her life. To be honest, I've grown used to it." Tatiana sighed. "Out of sheer exasperation, I've tried to have her assassinated too, but she's grown too strong and wary for me to get anyone close enough to do it. And somehow, she has gathered her Hounds. They are utterly loyal to her."

Pia finished her meal and set the pasta bowl aside. Then, because she couldn't resist, she asked, "When was Dragos at Isabeau's Court?"

"Some time before I got pregnant, but now that I think about it, not too much earlier." Frowning, Tatiana set her uneaten meal aside as well and wiped her fingers with her napkin, as fastidious as a cat. She said, "Dragos didn't lose his memory from the contagion, did he?"

Pia stopped moving. For a moment, she didn't breathe, as her mind raced frantically around, searching for a way to deflect or misdirect.

But now that the Queen had flat out said the truth, her options had turned slim to none. The thing about shadows and misdirection was, once someone started to disbelieve the magic, their power dissipated like so much smoke.

She had almost begun to believe that they had tap-danced well enough that they were going to be able to keep all their secrets.

As her hesitation went on a bit too long, the Queen asked gently, "Was it the head injury? The news down-played his accident this summer, but of course the scar on his forehead is quite visible."

God, she hoped Dragos would forgive her for this. Pia met the other woman's gaze and said directly, "Yes."

Tatiana blinked. Clearly she hadn't expected such a straightforward response. "I see."

"He's going to hate that I told you that," she said dryly.

Long eyelashes fell, obscuring the expression in the other woman's eyes. "You don't need to let him know that you told me."

Pia wasn't about to play that game. "Oh, yes, I do. We have no secrets between us. Ever."

Tatiana acknowledged that by lifting one shoulder. "That's always the wisest course in a marriage. It's an especially wise course of action to take as Dragos's mate."

"Well, it isn't a tactical maneuver," she replied, glancing out the window. Dragos had eaten some of the food on the tray and pushed the rest aside. Now he lay on his back, eyes closed, hands folded across his flat, lean stomach. Despite the thick chains circling his wrists and ankles, he looked quite comfortable. She smiled to herself. "We trust each other. So, he'll be annoyed with me, but he'll get over it."

Envy flashed across the other woman's face, or at least she thought it did. It had vanished in the next instant, so she couldn't tell. Tatiana asked, "Do you know how much memory he's lost?"

"At first, his memory loss was total. But, thank God, that didn't last more than a few days. Now, almost all of it has returned. Everything that matters to me, at least. He has a few pockets of long-term memory loss, but mostly, those are historical events. It's really just a fluke that the whole thing has come up. If we hadn't been so preoccupied with—with other things, I don't think there would have even been a misstep." She smoothed her fingers along the edges of the chair cushion. "Can you tell me what Dragos was doing at the Seelie Court?"

"To be honest, I don't really know," Tatiana replied. "He was a recurring guest for several seasons. He and Isabeau seemed to have this ongoing thing."

Utterly flummoxed, Pia stared at the other woman.

Thing? What did Tatiana mean by *thing*?

One thought after the other tumbled through her mind. Had they been enemies? *Lovers?* Dragos was older than sin. She had known for a fact that he'd had sex before, and probably quite a lot of it at some point or other, because he knew how to do such wise, wickedly inventive things that made her eyes pop out of her head, and she was quite sure they hadn't exhausted all of his repertoire of tricks yet.

But knowing something had happened and coming up against the reality of it were two different things entirely.

She wasn't jealous at the thought. Not exactly. Dragos was hers, totally, but she did feel sour and unsettled.

The only way to get more information was to pump Tatiana for it, because Dragos wouldn't be able to tell her anything, even if he wanted to. She asked, "What do you mean, they had an ongoing *thing*? Do you mean they had an affair?"

"I don't know," Tatiana replied. "They might have, but I never knew anything for sure. Even then, I was marginalized at her Court, and I was certainly not privy to any confidences. I remember they sort of smilingly poked at each other verbally, and she seemed to be fascinated by him. And I had no idea how to read him. It had something of a flirtatious hint to it, but there was also this edge, like maybe they hadn't yet decided whether or not they were enemies. She once called him 'that damn inquisitive dragon.' I always wondered if he was either trying to get information from her, or perhaps he was searching for something. Maybe he'll remember in time."

"Maybe," Pia said. Inwardly, she doubted it. He had recovered most of his lost memories within a few days after the accident, and now, the more time passed, the less likely it was that he would remember.

"Well, if you have anything to do with Isabeau, be careful. I cannot say if she and Dragos parted on friendly terms or not, and as you have seen for yourself, she is a vicious and relentless enemy."

"I appreciate the warning." Rubbing her forehead, she wondered how Aryal, Quentin and Shane were doing. No news might be good news. Of course, it might not too. Quentin had seemed pretty certain that Morgan would kick their asses. She muttered, "Why is Isabeau's Chief Hound called Morgan of the Fae?"

"Because Morgan lives at Isabeau's Court, but he isn't actually Light Fae himself. Neither Shane nor I are quite sure what he is, although I make a point of not getting close enough to him to find out. He seems human, but he's also hundreds of years old, which of course no normal human could achieve." Tatiana had tensed while she talked. Now she looked unsettled as well. "If he has human blood in him, he also has something else—either Elder Races blood, or perhaps some kind of magical Power—that has prolonged his life. Not much frightens me, but he does."

A trickle of real fear for Quentin and Aryal ran down Pia's spine. She wished they would get in touch somehow, but of course they would be too busy to call, and Dragos's telepathy was down.

While they talked, she kept part of her attention on the quiet, sunny afternoon outside, which was how she saw what happened next.

The quiet scene erupted. In place of the large, black-haired man lying prone on the lawn, an immense bronze dragon appeared, with the bronze coloring darkening to black at the tips of his long talons, tail and gigantic wings. His sudden appearance knocked the two Hummers sidelong. Looking down at his body, the dragon shook himself like a dog, and his chains fell away.

Fierce joy shot through Pia, as strong as a sunburst.

Guards shouted in both surprise and alarm, causing Tatiana to spin in her seat and stare wide-eyed out the window.

The dragon mantled his massive wings, looked at the guards and said, "If you shoot at me now, you're only going to piss me off."

Surging to her feet, Tatiana strode to the French doors and yanked them open. She shouted, "Any fool that shoots at him will face disciplinary action!"

The dragon strode to the verandah. It took him three steps.

Grinning, Pia pushed to her feet and poked her head around Tatiana. "Hi, baby," she said. "Good to see you."

"Good to be here," Dragos said. He folded his wings into place and cocked his head to look under the verandah roof at her with one golden eye. "I'm going hunting. Okay with you?"

"Everything's great with me," she told him, beaming.

He told her, "Take your medicine."

"I will." Telepathically, she said, *I love you.*

Love you too. Be back later.

With that, he wheeled, crouched and launched into the air.

✧　✧　✧

DRAGOS HAD TRIED to shapeshift every ten or fifteen minutes. When he finally did connect with his Wyr form and shift, he felt the last of the contagion burn away.

Now, he tore through the air, fierce eagerness fueling his flight. He said telepathically to Aryal, *Where are you?*

Whoa, she exclaimed. *You're telepathizing!*

While I appreciate your gift for the obvious, he drawled. *I would rather know your location.*

South Harbor Boulevard, she said briefly. *Near the waterfront. There's a large herd of zombies here, Dragos. The Hounds are here too, behind them, driving them forward at us. They're using them as shields while throwing attack spells at us.*

Zombies?

He coughed out an unamused laugh. That was as good a word for them as any.

He told her, *I'm coming in hot. Tell the others to get out.*

Hells yes! As far as I'm concerned, you can torch them all. Most of them are half eaten—they couldn't survive any kind of antidote or reversion anyway.

That's what I saw in the group that attacked me. He flew west, as hard as he could. *Shoreline's in sight now.*

Quentin and Shane's forces are retreating. They're in an SUV, headed south.

Got it.

The sun hung lower in the sky since he had been chained, reigning over the western horizon and sparkling on the vast water. As he neared the waterfront area, he felt blasts of magic from the battle.

A winged figure shot into the air and swooped. It was Aryal. She held an automatic weapon and sprayed the area below her with gunfire. He caught a glimpse of flying black hair, piercing gray eyes, and her angular, hawkish face.

A deadly spell burst upward like a firework at her, but dipping one wing, she rolled to the side and let herself fall through the air, and the spell shot past her harmlessly.

The dragon smiled to himself. As usual, she was utterly fearless.

Compared to his size, though, she was like a two-seater aircraft. He told her, *Stay out of my way.*

Flipping, she righted herself and flew south after the SUV.

In the next moment, he was on the scene.

The infected herd was large, and its members as fast as the ones who had attacked him earlier. But they weren't fast enough to outrun him.

As the dragon dove, he opened his jaws and let all of his anger boil out. Fire spewed onto the scene. In just a pass or two of his wings, he had shot past. Wheeling, he turned and dove again, laying fire over four industrial blocks.

Only when he felt sure that he had covered the area thoroughly did he pull up to land in the middle of the hot blaze. The dangerous, pathetic figures of the infected collapsed almost immediately.

From the ground, it looked as though the world was on fire. It suited the dragon's apocalyptic mood. He strolled down the street. The flames were so hot, the asphalt underneath his talons grew soft and sticky, then caught fire. At times like this, when he was enraged and civilization had fallen completely away, he thought he could burn down the world and never miss it.

When that happened, he could hear a quiet voice at the back of his mind.

You could do it, brother, Death whispered. *We could do it together.*

These days, however, when he heard that quiet, far-off voice, he shook away the lure that Death held for him. There was too much buoyant life that surrounded him, and love. His mate. His son. His new, unknown child, as mysterious as an unexplored land.

Maybe we could, the dragon said to the quiet voice. *But we won't today.*

Up ahead, the figure of a man walked toward him, through the flames.

Dragos stilled, and his eyes narrowed. Dragon fire burned hotter than almost any other blaze, save the sun's, but the figure did not appear to be affected.

As the man neared, his features and form became distinguishable. He wore tailored black clothes, leather gloves and a leather suit jacket that could, Dragos noted, hide any number of weapons. He was tall and wide-shouldered, and moved with the kind of liquid athleticism that Dragos associated with his Wyr soldiers, but this was no Wyr.

He looked like a human man in his midthirties, deeply tanned, with chestnut hair and clear hazel eyes, and a strong, contemplative, even sad, face. And he carried so much Power, he felt like a walking, talking nuclear bomb.

The dragon's hackles rose.

"Lord Cuelebre," the man greeted him in a calm

voice that Dragos could hear perfectly well over the roar of the flames around them. He spoke with a Welsh accent. "Unfortunately, you managed to kill all my compatriots before I could reach them in time. You are not supposed to be here."

Dragos didn't recognize the male. Perhaps he would have, once upon a time, before his head injury. Falling so unexpectedly into that hole in his memory made him rage even more.

So he took an educated guess.

"Morgan," the dragon growled. The man did not deny the name. "You are not supposed to be here either. You started the contagion." The dragon stalked closer. "And when the Light Fae came close to eradicating it, you worked to spread it."

"My Queen commands, and I am compelled to obey," Morgan said, inclining his head and offering a slight, courteous bow.

"Did your Queen compel you to destroy all the Elder Races?" Dragos barked.

As the dragon drew nearer, the other male turned slightly to walk at an angle, until they were circling each other like adversaries, while everything around them burned. At Dragos's accusation, Morgan tilted his head. "Her quarrel is with this Light Fae demesne. It does not involve you, or the rest of the Elder Races."

"Quite the contrary," the dragon hissed. Lunging forward, he snapped at the other male, who leaped back, faster and more fluid than Dragos had believed possible. Morgan gestured, and a wall of Power slammed between them, shimmering from the fire. "It involves me. My mate. And it involves any race that carries a hint of Power. Both human and different Elder Races can be infected by the contagion. Your creatures attacked me. One of them broke my skin. I started to turn."

The other male frowned, his clear hazel gaze sharp. "You were susceptible?"

"For a brief time, I was." Dragos pushed at the wall of Power, seeking a way to get through. "And I am not susceptible to any illness. Magically inclined humans have caught it and turned. This contagion is utter *madness*. It will destroy all of us if it is allowed to spread."

Morgan closed his eyes, and his face tightened. "She swore it would only kill the Light Fae in this demesne."

Only kill the Light Fae? He spoke of eradicating hundreds, if not thousands of people.

"Well, the bitch was wrong," Dragos snarled. He clawed at the wall of Power, and the tips of his talons screeched down the shimmering barrier like nails on a chalkboard. As he tried to stalk around it, the wall shifted, keeping pace with him. "You have something that creates this hell. A magic item, or a vial of something. Where is it? *Give it to me!*"

To the dragon's astonishment, Morgan reached inside his leather suit jacket and pulled out an amulet.

Even through the dragonfire and the sorcerous Power that Morgan exuded, the amulet seemed to radiate an aura of blackness.

It wasn't as strong as a Deus Machina, or God Machine. There were only seven Machines in the world, and they could not be destroyed. Back at the beginning of the world, the seven gods of the Elder Races had thrown something of themselves into the world to enact their will through the ages.

Dragos had encountered God Machines before. He knew how to identify them, and while this amulet was no Machine, still, it was imbued with a touch of Death's Power. Dragos might not be susceptible to any illness, but Death's Power could still touch him. Theoretically, he could die, and the fact that he had been susceptible to the contagion reinforced that theory.

Dragos stilled. "Where did you get that?"

"My Queen gave it to me and ordered me to use it," Morgan told him. "But it does more harm than she promised."

He tossed it high in the air, and the amulet fell to the ground on Dragos's side of the barrier. Dragos bared his teeth. "What happened to the 'my Queen commands, and I am compelled to obey' shit?"

Morgan raised his eyebrows. "She did command, and I have obeyed. But now I am done."

With that, he turned and walked away. Within a few steps, the fire appeared to swallow him whole. At the same moment, the barrier melted away.

Scooping up the amulet in one giant claw, Dragos lunged after the other man, but Morgan had disappeared completely from his sight and his senses.

After stalking around the area for several moments, eventually he gave up the hunt. Instead, he turned his attention to the deadly amulet he clutched in one claw.

The amulet was made of a large, faceted onyx stone that reflected the dying fire.

Normally, onyx didn't work well for holding magic. The harder jewels, like diamonds and rubies, worked the best for containing magic. Whoever had created the amulet had had a particular flare for Death magic.

As partial as the dragon was to items of jewelry, there were some things too dangerous to hoard.

He concentrated his Power on the amulet, working to crush the magic even as he squeezed his claw to crush the stone.

At first both magic and stone resisted. It was incredibly strong. Drawing on more Power, and all of his strength, he gritted massive teeth and strained until he felt an invisible *snap*, and the onyx broke. He crushed it until there was nothing left but dust.

Chapter Ten

After he destroyed the amulet, he turned his concentration to the fire that still blazed in places. Pulling hard, he drew the flames back into him. For a brief time he was immersed in fire. Closing his eyes and breathing deeply, he let his consciousness be immersed in the brilliant heat.

When it subsided, he contacted Aryal telepathically. *The herd of infected here are all incinerated. I killed a couple of Hounds, but I didn't manage to kill Morgan. He's gone.*

Too bad, the harpy said. Vindictiveness tinged her voice, like the sharp edge of her claws. *You okay?*

Yes. Morgan gave me the source of the contagion. It was magical in nature. I've destroyed it. As he talked, he launched into the air. *I'm going back to Tatiana's. Work with Shane until you're sure the rest of the infected are burned. I might have destroyed the source, but they can still spread the contagion through their bites. Report back when you are all confident the job is done.*

Understood.

There was no way Dragos was going to show up at Tatiana's without making sure he had gotten rid of any lingering traces of the amulet. Flying due west for a half a mile or so, he dove into the ocean until he reached the sandy floor. Scooping up clawfuls of sand, he surfaced again and scrubbed at himself until he felt certain that he was entirely clean.

Only then did he head back to Bel Air, winging through the distance at a tired, leisurely pace.

This time, he landed a couple of blocks down the street and shapeshifted back into a man so that he could walk the rest of the way toward the large, sprawling mansion. The sun had not yet set, but it was low enough in the sky that it had gone down below the silhouette of the surrounding houses, throwing deep shadows across the lawns and the street.

As he walked, he admired the ultra-landscaped lawns in front of the other Bel Air properties. He said in Pia's head, *I'm so glad we don't have a lot of flowers and other plant froufrou around our house. I'd never feel comfortable about shapeshifting, in case I accidentally knocked shit over with my tail, or trampled a rose garden.*

Which is exactly why we don't have all that. There was a smile in Pia's voice as she replied. *Between you, Liam, all of the sentinels and various other Wyr, if we had any kind of fancy garden, it would get trampled to dirt inside of a month. If you can chitchat lawn care, should I take it to mean that whatever situation was out there is taken care of?*

Yes, you should. I'm walking up to Tatiana's house right now. I'll tell you about it later. He paused. He hadn't had anything to do with either the interior design or landscaping of the house. Pia had done all of that, and she had thought everything through very thoroughly. He told her, *You are a wise woman.*

Pleasure warmed her voice. *I do have my moments, don't I? But then … I have other moments too. Dragos, I have to confess something. Tatiana nailed me down about your memory loss, and I couldn't find a way to wiggle out of admitting the truth.*

Oh, for fuck's sake, he sighed. He felt a brief impulse to strangle the Light Fae Queen. *How much does she know?*

Well … pretty much an abbreviated version of everything. I never would have volunteered to tell her anything, but she had already guessed that the contagion hadn't really messed with your thinking. She told me quite a story, both how she and Isabeau became estranged, and also something of your time at the Seelie Court.

Briefly, he wrestled with his pride, and pragmatism won. *Did she give you any indication what I was doing at Isabeau's Court?*

Not really. She indulged in some speculation, but she didn't know anything for sure. She said you and Isabeau sort of flirted, but sort of acted edgy around each other. She didn't know if you were ever lovers, or even if you had parted on friendly terms.

As Pia talked, he grew close enough that Tatiana's mansion came into view.

He told her, *I don't remember any other lover but you.*

I don't believe you.

I don't. I know the facts of other lovers, but all the real, visceral memory, or any emotion has burned away. Those lovers happened to someone else, the man I was before I met you.

She had stepped out onto the lawn. Eva and a couple of vigilant Light Fae guards stood with her, but as the Light Fae guards were actually guarding her, he didn't mind them so much. When they saw him, they didn't draw their weapons. Another win for the day.

Pia saw him at the same time. He started walking faster, and she gathered her skirt up in one hand and broke into a run. She flew down the driveway, and the eager light on her face was simply everything.

She hit him in the chest with her full weight, flinging her arms around his neck. Laughing, he spread his feet wide to absorb the impact and snatched her close. She held him so tightly, she damn near strangled him, and he knew he all but crushed her ribs.

Burying his face into her neck, he growled, "I *hated* not being able to touch you."

"I know. I felt the same." Greedily, she stroked the back of his head, and his shoulders. "You're okay? Quentin and Aryal—they're okay?"

"They're fine. From the way Aryal talked, I believe Shane is fine too, but I don't know anything about Shane's men." He rubbed his face in her hair, tightened his arms until she squeaked, then eased his hold on her. "Come on, let's go inside. That way I can tell this story just once."

Together, they turned and walked to the house. He kept his arm around her shoulders, and she slipped an arm around his waist. She told him telepathically, *I gave myself the injection.*

He had no longer been worried, but still, the confirmation lightened his spirits. *Good. That means you're going to feel tired and achy—or do you feel that way already?*

I'm pretty tired, she admitted.

She never complained about it. Not once. Everything

she said about the pregnancy was filled with a positive attitude and eagerness for the new arrival. He replied, *I take it that means you do feel achy too.*

She shrugged. *It's okay.*

He tightened his arm around her shoulders and said aloud, "And that means you need to go to bed soon. See, I'm figuring out your encoded messages."

She gave him a brief, laughing glance.

Tatiana herself came to the front door, meeting them as they were about to step in. She smiled at him. "I just heard from Bailey. They have a few areas they need to scour, but she thinks the tide has turned now."

"It has," Dragos said.

"Come back to the family room and tell me what happened." Turning, she led the way to the back of the house.

Settling on one of the couches, with Pia curled at his side, he told Tatiana and Pia about the encounter with Morgan, and the amulet, which he had destroyed.

"I don't know how she could let something like that loose in the world," Tatiana murmured, looking ill. "We skirted so close to catastrophe. As it is, I've lost hundreds of my people."

Something teased at the back of his mind, and he paused, waiting to see what came of the sensation. It felt like memory ... or almost a memory. Then, in the next instance, the feeling was gone. Frustrated, he shook his head.

"Isabeau needs to die," he said crisply. Pia rested her head on his shoulder, and he pressed a brief kiss to her forehead. "But then, so many people do. And the reality of it is, she's very well guarded. She has full control over her Other land, and her Hounds appear to be completely loyal to her. And Morgan is—formidable. I'll never understand how obsessive people can command such fanatic loyalty."

"Well, she has more than her fair share of the Light Fae charisma, which would help." Tatiana's gaze fell to Pia. Suddenly her face softened, and she smiled. Looking back up at Dragos, she put a finger to her lips.

He raised his eyebrows. Then he tilted his head to look into Pia's face. She had fallen deeply asleep. Her lashes cast long shadows on the curve of her cheeks, and her soft, full mouth had gone lax.

She whispered, "I remember those days too, when I was pregnant."

"Tatiana," he said in a soft, gentle voice, so as not to disturb his sleeping wife, "if you try to kick me out tonight, I'll make it my personal mission to tear Bel Air down around your ears."

"I wouldn't dream of it," Tatiana said quietly. "You have helped us tremendously today, and I am very grateful. We still need to adhere to the terms of the diplomatic pact, but I think we can get away with you staying one night. And frankly, what you choose to do with the rest of your week is none of my business. I'm certainly not going to be spying on you, should you and Pia meet up somewhere while she is out and about this week."

"Thank you," he said, relaxing.

"For tonight, I'll have one of my guards show you where her suite is."

The Queen stood, and he gathered Pia's warm, soft weight into his arms and stood also. Then he paused. *One other thing,* he said telepathically.

Tatiana paused as well, and looked at him inquiringly.

Don't poke at my wife about her Wyr form, he said. He gave her one of his hardest warning looks. *I mean it, Tatiana. Leave her alone about it. She told me you had questioned her in D.C. Her Wyr form is shy by nature, and in the early days of our mating, it was a real strain for her to contemplate being with me. She gave up a lot to be my mate. She's had to adapt to the limelight, and I won't have her bullied or pressured over it.*

The Light Fae Queen pursed her lips in a disappointed moue. *Oh, very well.* She paused. *By the way, I've heard a preliminary report from my doctors who are studying your blood samples. They're quite electrified at what they're finding. They think they've isolated the contagion and might be able to develop something from it, which will be hugely useful if there are any more outbreaks. Also, apparently your blood is intensely magical in nature, but then nobody is surprised by that. And there's something else—something truly unique, and they don't know quite what to make of it.*

Pia had already tried to heal him before his blood had been drawn. Was it something from her, or was it something inherent to him? Had she healed him after all?

Maybe the protocol had suppressed her nature but had not entirely negated it. Her blood might have worked, but very slowly. Or perhaps he had thrown off the effects of the contagion, himself.

They would never know for sure.

For now, he injected scorn into his mental voice. *Tell me, have any of your doctors ever studied dragon's blood before?*

Her brows twitched together. *You know they have not.*

He snorted. *Then of course it's truly unique.*

Cocking her head, she smiled wryly. *You do have a point.*

He reached out for Grym. *I hear they've isolated the contagion.*

They sure have, and in record time, Grym said. *There's a celebratory air right now in this lab.*

Time to destroy all the blood samples. Make sure they're incinerated, so that not a single cell is left.

You got it. Oh, the weeping and gnashing of teeth that will shortly commence.

Dragos smiled to himself. They hadn't preserved every one of their secrets. But they had managed to preserve the most important one.

Then Tatiana stepped to the door, opened it, and he carried Pia through to the hallway, and up to the suite.

✦   ✦   ✦

PIA WALKED ALONG her favorite trail, enjoying the fall colors.

Wait a minute. She had already done this before. Remembering jolted her so that she realized she was dreaming.

Tilting her head, she walked slowly and listened for a small, stealthy rustle. Sure enough, she heard it, behind her and a little to the left.

She didn't turn around or do anything to spook her small shadow. Instead, pretending to ignore it, she walked along slowly, thinking.

Soon, she came to an area where the trail opened up and the land flattened to form a high, grassy meadow atop a bluff that overlooked the land's long decline. Eventually that decline would lead to their house, which was half hidden by the surrounding trees. Beyond the house lay the flat blue shimmer of the nearby lake.

Strolling through the small meadow, she picked a spot and settled cross-legged on the ground, looking over the countryside. The scene was beautiful, with rolling hills covered with the brilliant gold, yellow and vermillion of the fall foliage. She loved everything about upstate New York in the autumn.

A small rustle might be approaching. Happiness filled her. Cocking her head, she listened to the slight, cautious sounds behind her and fought not to laugh. What would her shadow decide to do now?

Something sharp poked her in the lower back, over her left kidney. She swept a hand behind her to move the stick, or weed, or whatever it was, but her hand encountered nothing but air.

Hm.

The sharp something poked her again.

Moving gently, so as to not frighten the wary shadow away, she twisted to look over her shoulder.

Underneath the slender spire of a horn, fierce gold eyes looked back at her.

Oh, holy gods. She froze. She didn't even dare to

breathe.

The small creature standing just behind her shoulder was ... was ...

It was small like a newborn foal, all gangly legs and overlarge head, with a narrow, racy body. And it was dark bronze all over, almost exactly the same shade that Dragos was in his dragon form, with the colors darkening to black at the legs, nose and tail.

And it had that slender horn at the middle of its forehead. The horn would lengthen and sharpen as it grew to adulthood, but for now, it was short and well suited for a baby's developing neck muscles.

"Oh, Stinkpot," she whispered. "You're so beautiful."

And so frightening.

This was the creature that carried the fiery Power that Liam had sensed. Those eyes, that coloring, were so like Dragos. If its personality was as fiery as its Power, it would have a royal temper. A temper that might even override all the instincts of its Wyr nature, instincts that would urge it to run and hide, or take the less obvious path to avoid detection and danger.

Swishing its tail, Stinkpot bent its head to nibble at the yellowing grass. While it acted like it was distracted, Pia carefully, carefully tightened her stomach muscles and leaned back to see if she could catch a glimpse between its slender, gangly legs.

Oh my God. Stinkpot was male. Delight, wonder and sheer terror clanged through her head like a three-bell alarm.

She whispered, "Are you okay if I pick you up now, darling?"

At the sound of her voice, Stinkpot flicked an ear but didn't appear to be otherwise concerned. Moving slowly and gently, she twisted around to stroke his neck. His body was that of a newborn foal, but he carried the promise of power in the regal arch of his neck, and in the deep width of his chest.

He would be fast, she knew. Faster than almost anybody else, and he would be able to run for miles without tiring. She could see it all too well in her mind's eye. He would be talented at running all right, but instead of running away from danger, he would run straight toward it.

Stinkpot shifted and reached, as if to nibble at another blade of grass. It also happened to bring his neck closer underneath her hand, so that she could scratch more skin.

"I see what you're about now, young man," she crooned gently. "And I already know that you're going to like keeping your secrets. Are you going to be sneaky too like your daddy?"

He let out a *whuffle*, as if agreeing, and she couldn't hold back any longer. Reaching around him, she picked him up and gathered him close. He didn't protest or struggle. As she settled him in her lap, he folded those ridiculous, overlong legs and tucked his head in the crook of her arm. Bending over him, she buried her face in the thick, coarse hair of his mane.

Funny how love works. Peanut had stolen her heart,

and she adored Liam with all of her being. Now Stinkpot stole her heart all over again.

Both her sons were thieves, yet somehow she felt her heart still in her chest, beating hard from wonder, and it was full to bursting.

A large hand cupped her hip, traveled up the curve of her torso and flattened against the middle of her chest. Dragos murmured in her ear, "Pia, it's all right. You're just having a nightmare. Wake up."

As she startled, the dream vanished.

"*Ssh*, calm down." Dragos's voice was slow, deep and easy. He kissed the back of her neck. "Your heart is racing ninety miles an hour."

"Mm," she croaked, her voice rusty from sleep. Lifting her head off the pillow and squinting, she looked around to get her bearings.

They were in bed together, in her suite at Tatiana's residence. The room lay in deep shadows, so it was some time in the middle of the night. Somehow she had lost her clothing, and Dragos had too. She knew who the culprit was for that. He spooned her from behind, under the bedcovers, his larger, harder body providing a protective shell around her.

Their position was so familiar, so necessary, that even though they were still in southern California, a sense of well-being flowed through her, along with a feeling of being home.

Stretching, she yawned and twisted around to cuddle closer against him. As she rested her cheek against his warm, bare skin, she let her fingers follow the pattern of dark, silky hair that fanned across his wide, bare chest.

He cupped the side of her face, cradling her, and she felt warm, relaxed, completely protected and surrounded.

"Does Tatiana know you're here?" she mumbled.

"Yes." His deep voice was a quiet rumble in his chest. "We both agreed the circumstances of the day had been unusual enough that nobody would have a problem if I stayed for tonight. Are you still up for visiting the rest of the week with her? We can call this whole thing quits and go home in the morning, if you'd rather."

"And have to possibly come back again? Not on your life." Yawning again, she rubbed the sleep out of her eyes. "There's only six more days to go, and then the whole damn thing is over. Although I shudder to think what tomorrow will hold. What do you think—flood, fire or act of the gods?"

He snorted and pressed his mouth to her forehead. "What were you dreaming about?"

Remembering, she smiled with a small wordless croon. "It wasn't a nightmare. I was dreaming about Stinkpot."

"Really?" A smile entered his voice. "I'm sorry I woke you, then. Your heart was racing so hard, it woke me up."

"S'okay." Rubbing her face against his skin, she murmured in his head, *Do you want to know what I dreamed, or do you want to be surprised?*

You can surprise me right now. Easing her gently back on the bed, he kissed her lightly.

Telepathizing in bed was one of her very favorite

things to do. They could have entire conversations while kissing like horny teenagers. The only problem with it was she lost control of her train of thought. That, and often her verbal skills degenerated to things like: *Holy shit, do that again. My God! Ah, so good … please—please—*

Smiling at the thought, she inserted the palm of one hand between their lips so that he couldn't distract her into incoherency. She told him, *Stinkpot is a gorgeous, wary, sneaky little boy. He's got your coloring and my Wyr form. And from what Liam was picking up, possibly your Power and temper.*

Dragos froze. She could just about feel the wheels turning in his head. After a moment, he said, *Good gods.*

Terrified glee suffused her. Sticking her tongue between her teeth, she fizzed like uncorked champagne. *Raising that kid is going to kill us both dead.*

Goddamn, Dragos muttered. *Just thinking about it might kill me dead. I can't wait to meet the little booger. He sounds amazing.*

He is, and I can't wait for you to meet him too. Sobering, she threw her arms around his neck. *I'm so happy you didn't turn. I think I might have gone a little crazy today. I had all these manic ideas about converting our basement into a big jail cell and keeping you chained up down there until I gave birth to Stinkpot, so that I could try to heal you then.*

It's okay. Everything is okay now. His arms closed around her tightly. *What do you remember of what I was telling Tatiana?*

Not much. Burying her face against him, she inhaled his healthy, clean scent. *I fell asleep a few minutes after we sat on the couch.*

With a few quick, concise sentences, he filled her in on the conversation. *The lab has the contagion isolated, and Grym let me know about forty-five minutes ago that he personally destroyed all the blood samples. Quentin and Aryal are still out with Shane. They're combing through neighborhoods street by street, but they haven't found any more infected for a few hours now. Right now, they just want to err on the side of caution before calling an end to the search.*

She lay still, absorbing the news. *And you're sure Morgan has gone?*

I'm certain he has, after giving me the amulet. He said he had done what he was commanded to do. Dragos paused. His voice turned darker and edged. *I should have known who he was. I should have remembered him. He's very dangerous, Pia. He walked through my dragonfire unscathed, and he blocked every attempt I made to get at him.*

If he's not Light Fae, then what is he? Could you tell?

He shook his head. *There was too much fire burning all around us, so I couldn't get his scent. Just from looking at him, I think he has some human blood. But he's clearly not fully human. He was faster and could jump much farther than a human could.*

She shivered. *Now I understand why you've been so obsessive about trying to recover those lost memories.*

You never know. Something may still come back to me.

He didn't sound convinced of that, and neither was she. The longer he went without recovering those memories, the less likely it was that he would ever recall them. Dr. Shaw had made it very clear. They would have to live with the consequences of that fact and be grateful that he had recovered as many memories as he had.

Shrugging it off, Dragos leaned over her again. *Enough about him. We have the rest of tonight before your week resumes, and I intend on taking full advantage of it.*

Gladly, she surrendered to the change in focus. *Ooh,* she crooned, running her fingers lightly along the powerful bulk of his shoulders. The silhouette of his body was darker than the rest of the room, as he eclipsed the night. From the darkest part of the shadow, she caught a glint of his intent gold eyes. *What do you have in mind?*

It was too dark for her to see his smile, but she could hear it in his voice. *Probably too many things for the amount of time that we've got, but you never know. I'm an ambitious man.*

Settling back against her pillow, she whispered, "Let's take everything on your list one at a time and see where we get."

"Item one," he growled quietly. The intense shadow moved, and suddenly his mouth was on hers, hard, hot and demanding.

Desire surged through her veins, burning away logic and common sense. In that moment, he could have asked her for anything, and she would have agreed gladly.

Thrusting his tongue into her mouth, he ran a greedy hand down the curves of her body, pinching and flicking at her nipple with a thumbnail and kneading the soft, full flesh of her breast, while the hard length of his erection pressed against her hip.

It could never be boring between them. All their lovemaking over the last eighteen months had conditioned her to associate his touch with such extreme pleasures that all he had to do was touch her hand and give her that keen, hard smile of his, and she melted into liquid heat. Her body was greedy for it, for him, and the thought of what they would do—what he would do to her—made the muscles in her thighs start to shake.

I can smell it on you, he muttered in her head. *Your arousal. It makes me so damn hungry. You're already wet, aren't you?*

Uh huh, she whimpered.

Wiggling under the heavy weight of his large body, she ran her own hand along the long length of his torso. His hot skin felt like silk wrapped over iron muscles. When her questing fingers found the tip of his cock, they both groaned. His own mounting arousal had caused moisture to bead at the slit. Using the ball of her thumb, she took the moisture and rubbed it along the broad, mushroom head, until he hissed and grabbed at her wrist.

Sometimes he could let her tease him, and then other times, like now, his dominant side took over. She was more than happy to go with either scenario. Pinning her wrists on either side of her head, he growled telepathically, *Open your legs.*

Hunger pulsed. God, she loved it when he got growly and autocratic. Arching in a stretch that rubbed her torso against his, she put her mouth lightly against his and whispered, "Make me."

He stilled. Then it was as if she had thrown a lit match on a lake of gasoline. Everything went up in flames.

Yanking her legs apart, he settled into place at the intimate bowl of her pelvis. When she would have reached to help guide his erection into place, he snatched at her wrists again. This time he pinned them over her head with one massive hand.

Testing the strength of his hold, she struggled to get free, although not that seriously. He liked it when she struggled. It struck at some deep predatory part of him that they both recognized and embraced as part of their extensive repertoire of love play.

As she twisted underneath his weight, the growl that came out of his throat was so low and aggressive, the tiny hairs at the back of her neck raised. God, that sound made her wetter than ever. She wanted to take his cock into her mouth and pump him dry. She wanted him to thrust inside her, and thrust, and thrust....

Restlessly she tried to wrap her legs around his hips, but with his free hand, he thrust her back down on the bed. Then, keeping her pinned, he bent to suckle at her breasts, first one then the other, flicking and teasing the stiff peaks of her nipples with his tongue in between drawing hard so that sensations sizzled down the length of her body.

The hunger for his touch grew harder to control, throbbing in time with the pull of his mouth. Physically aching for his touch, she whimpered and started to struggle in earnest, but he wouldn't release her.

"*Dragos*," she hissed urgently.

In response, he lifted his hand from her pelvis.

Only to lay the broad, hard palm over her mouth.

Of course he wasn't gagging her, not really, since they could telepathize, but the move was so dark and primitive, she almost came right then and there, without him ever touching her clitoris.

Shaken at her own response to the maneuver, she groaned. The sound was small and muffled against the palm of his hand. Her breathing came hard and fast, the expelled air from her nostrils hitting his skin in short, hard puffs.

He paused. He was breathing hard too. She could hear the rasp of it, a tiny, raw sound that told her how close he was to losing control. He asked her telepathically, *Okay?*

I almost came just now without you touching me! she exclaimed. *How okay do you think I am?*

The grip he had on her mouth softened. *Does it ache?*

Yes! She struggled against the hold he kept on her wrists.

Bending down, he whispered in her ear, "How badly do you want me?"

She sobbed, *So much! Dragos—please ...*

And there it happened again. The heat between them became so intense, her verbal skills flew out the window.

The hard hand at her mouth moved away, and he released her wrists. Sliding down the bed, he murmured, *I'll make it better.*

She knew what he intended to do, and if she let him put his mouth on her, he would work at her until she screamed and flailed endlessly before he finally took his pleasure. While she loved those moments, this time she felt too impatient, too needy.

Before he could settle between her legs, she scrambled onto her hands and knees and told him, *I want you inside me—now.*

He could see better in the dark than she could. As she said the words, she arched in invitation. For a moment, the cool air-conditioning licked along her overheated bare skin. She could feel his gaze like a touch as he watched her. Then the darkest shadow in the room moved behind her to cover her with heat and hardness.

He positioned his cock at her entrance, rubbing himself on the passion soaked petals of her private flesh. As he did so, she hugged a pillow to herself and, bracing her weight on one elbow, reached between her legs to stroke his stiff length. As she touched him, his penis jerked.

Muttering a soft swear under his breath, he found her entrance and pushed in. No matter how many times they made love or just coupled together in wild, no-holds-barred monkey sex, she never grew tired of the sensation of his hard, thick cock entering her.

He gripped her by the hips and didn't stop pushing until he had seated himself to the root. Their ragged breathing played in counterpart as he gave her a moment to adjust. When he began to move, she buried her face in the pillow to muffle the needy sounds she made.

As he fucked her, he reached around to rub her aching clitoris, and her climax came with such abrupt savagery it tore her breath away. Sometimes the pleasure he gave her was almost too great, too sharp. It wrung her body out and destroyed her thinking.

As she shook from the force of the pleasure that rocked through her, he bit the back of her neck. Still pistoning inside her, still massaging the center of her pleasure. She didn't even have a chance to come down from the first peak before the second one slammed into her. Gripping his wrist as he worked her, she bucked and squealed.

Her thinking was destroyed. All she could do was hang on to him, while erotic images and impressions ran through her mind.

All the times they'd had sex. Rutted like the animals they were. Made love with gentleness and emotion. She knew the look in his eyes when she came, the combination of tenderness and intense male satisfaction. She knew how he looked when he came, feral and often inhuman, transported out of his own self-containment. There in the darkness, she saw all of his faces in her mind's eye, and they were all the face of the man she loved.

He bit her harder, fucked her harder. She could feel his teeth pressing on her skin and knew he would leave marks. The small pain combined with the pleasure, and drove her forward into yet another climax. This time she had no breath. All she could do was whine softly, a shaky, raw sound.

Then he paused, buried to the root inside her. She felt him begin to pulse and knew her own moment of intense female satisfaction. Whomever he had taken as lovers before in his very long life, now he was hers, entirely.

She had to say it to him. Licking swollen lips, she whispered, "You're mine. Mine."

He wrapped one arm around her, gently encircling her throat with his hand, taking total ownership of her with the gesture. Rocking against her pelvis, he murmured into the nape of her neck, "Until I take my last breath, and beyond."

Usually he was the one who descended into declarations of possessiveness, and she relished it every time. But whenever she felt the need to claim him as she had just now, he always gave himself to her, unreservedly.

Full of emotion, she reached up and behind her to cup the back of his head. He turned and pressed a kiss to her fingers.

"I don't want you to go in the morning," she complained softly.

Pulling away, he stretched out on the bed and pulled her into his arms. Her muscles felt like jelly, and she went down to him gladly.

As she settled against him, he wrapped his arms around her. "It's only six more days now, and I'll be nearby. And our night's not over yet. We're just going to take a little breather for a few moments."

"Sounds good," she said, face planted into his shoulder so that her words came out muffled. She didn't think she could sit up straight, let alone do something as sophisticated as walk to the bathroom. Light flooded the room, and she flinched with a gasp. He had turned on the bedside lamp. "Why did you do that? The dark was cozy."

"I have a present for you," he said.

She lifted her head to squint at him. "When on earth did you find time to get me a present?"

One corner of his hard mouth lifted. "I have my ways." He reached one long, bare arm to a pile of red and white that lay in a jumble by his cell phone. As he shook out the first piece, she realized it was a necklace. And oh lord, what a necklace! Fiery ruby red and sparks of light flowed over his long fingers.

Turned out, she did have the strength to sit up after all. "Oh my God," she breathed. As she held out her hands, he let the necklace settle into her grip. She examined the firebird. "This is breathtaking. Where did you get it?"

"A shop on Rodeo Drive," he said, his gaze resting on the brilliance lying in her cupped hands. "There are earrings too, and a bracelet."

"It's stunning." At first, when he gave her such extravagant gifts, she had felt uncomfortable, but he got such transparent pleasure out of it, she had set her own discomfort aside a long time ago. Now she simply reveled in the beauty of the necklace. Leaning forward, she kissed him. "I love it so much. Thank you!"

"My pleasure. Here, put it on." Sitting up, he helped her fasten the necklace. The firebird rested at the base of her throat. When she turned to face him, a smile creased his face. "You're as beautiful as I knew you would be, wearing it."

She knew his penchant for making love to her when

she wore jewels and she gave him a grin. "Is this on your list of things you wanted to get to, before morning?"

His smile widened. "You know me so well. I've been looking forward to it this whole hellish day."

At the mention of what had happened earlier, her expression darkened, but only for a moment. Reaching for his hand, she twined her fingers through his. "We dealt with it."

He squeezed her fingers. "And we'll continue to do so. The universe can bring it. We'll deal with whatever may happen together."

Something deeper than happiness took her over. Fulfillment, perhaps, along with a rush of love so deep for him, it made her eyes shimmer. "We always do."

With a tug, he pulled her down to him and kissed her. In the middle of the kiss, he rolled so that she lay on her back, and he sprawled across her. Lifting his head, he looked down at the firebird sparking against her skin, and his expression turned purposeful.

He said, "And now to get to the next item on my list."

"Ooh, goody." Eagerly, she surrendered to his kiss, and then she surrendered to a great many other things as well. Pleasure was foremost among them, along with laughter, and more love.

Among his many other qualities, her mate was a very thorough man.

Thank you!

Dear Readers,

Thank you for reading my novella, *Pia Does Hollywood*. Dragos, Pia and Liam Cuelebre are some of my favorite characters, and I'm delighted to share this new story with you. I hope you have as much fun visiting with them as I did!

Would you like to stay in touch and hear about new releases? You can:

- Sign up for my newsletter at: www.theaharrison.com
- Follow me on Twitter at @TheaHarrison
- Like my Facebook page at facebook.com/TheaHarrison

Reviews help other readers find the books they like to read. I appreciate each and every review, whether positive or negative.

Pia Does Hollywood is the second story in a three-story arc featuring Dragos, Pia and their son Liam. The first story is *Dragos Goes to Washington*, and the third is *Liam Takes Manhattan*. While each story is written so that it can be enjoyed individually, the reading experience will be stronger if you enjoy all three in order.

Happy reading!
Thea

Now Available

Dragos Goes to Washington
(A Novella of the Elder Races)

Dragos Cuelebre, Lord of the Wyr, needs to throw a party without maiming anyone.

That isn't exactly as easy as it might sound.

After the destructive events of the last eighteen months, the Elder Races are heading to Washington D.C. to foster peace with humankind. Not known for his diplomacy skills, Dragos must rely on his mate Pia to help navigate a battlefield of words and polite smiles rather than claws. With Dragos's mating instinct riding close to the surface, his temper is more volatile than ever and the threat of violence hovers in the air.

Then the human spouse of a prominent politician winds up murdered and Dragos and Pia must race against time to hunt down those behind it before they are held responsible for the crime.

For fans of *Dragon Bound* and *Lord's Fall*, the latest novella in the Elder Races holds passion, peril, political intrigue, and revelations that will change Dragos and Pia's lives forever.

Dragos Goes to Washington is the first part of a three-story series about Dragos, Pia, and their son Liam. Each story stands alone, but fans might want to read all three: *Dragos Goes to Washington*, *Pia Does Hollywood*, and *Liam Takes Manhattan*.

Now Available

Liam Takes Manhattan

(A Short Story of the Elder Races)

Warning: This story contains a major spoiler from SHADOW'S END (book #9, released December 1st, 2015). If readers do not want to be spoiled, they should read the stories in order of their release dates.

This is a short story (15,000 words or 50 pages) intended for readers of the Elder Races who enjoy Liam Cuelebre as a character.

Reeling from a deep loss, the magical prince of the Wyr, Dragos and Pia's son Liam Cuelebre, turns inward and withdrawn as he struggles to come to terms with who he is, along with the challenges that lie before him.

Hoping to ease his heartache and offer comfort, a concerned Dragos and Pia offer him a gift, something he has desired for a long time. Liam's response has a ripple effect across all of New York. Soon miracles of all kinds start arriving just in time for Christmas, along with a visit from a mysterious person who gives Liam hope and a vision of his future.

Liam Takes Manhattan is the third part of a three-story series about Pia, Dragos, and their son, Liam. Each story stands alone, but fans might want to read all three: *Dragos Goes to Washington*, *Pia Does Hollywood*, and *Liam Takes Manhattan*.

Look for these titles from Thea Harrison

18739020R00101

Printed in Great Britain
by Amazon